GHOST KILLER

GHOST KILLER

Book IX of the Evil Stryker Series

WES RAND

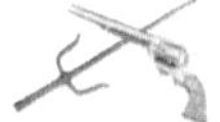

For my wife, Pamela.

"The past is never dead. It's not even past."

— WILLIAM FAULKNER

CHAPTER ONE

On the way to south Pescadero Beach, waves are broken up by rugged offshore rocks. Pescadero Creek flows into the sea, separating the northern sandy beach from the southern rocky shore. Sea lions and harbor seals frequent the southern area, sunning themselves before slipping back into the ocean to hunt.

On that late spring day, male sea lions had congregated on rock and sand rookeries to defend their territories. Among the one hundred or so sea lions on the beach below the twenty-foot escarpment, a pair of eight-hundred-pound males pounded and bit each other's necks to win the right to breed with females. The battle lasted half an hour with neither combatant willing to concede. Bloody wounds on both of their necks attested to the viciousness of the fight. Seldom fatal, the clashes were brutal. A female intruded on the epic brawl, snatching a trampled pup, but unfortunately, the pup is already dead.

A man sat astride a big roan horse above the cliff, impassively watching the melee below. When not on a horse, he stretched to a height of six feet, three inches, and tipped the scales at around two hundred pounds, give or take a couple of beers. Under the Stetson, black hair mingled with a few gray strands, hanging straight and to his shoulders. Wears his Mexican-style mustache drooped at the ends, and he had a week-old beard running along the jawline. His most striking facial features were the eyes, which were pale gray and intense, like the eyes of an eagle. Crow's feet radiated from the ghostly orbs. They are not laugh lines. The man called Stryker had not had an easy life.

He carried a.44 Colt Peacemaker as his sidearm and a Winchester.44 carbine in the saddle scabbard. He was handy with both. The straight razor in his rear pocket was for shaving–most of the time. It was the weapon he had down a pouch in the small of his back that sent a chill down men's spines. Called a sai, it was usually used in pairs, but he carried only one. The steel fork-like weapon had a long center tine and shorter tines on each side. All three were needle-sharp. Historically used as a farming tool by Asians, it was modified to defend against a sword. His uncle, a master in martial arts, taught him how to fight with it when he was a young boy in San Francisco. Men had died while staring at their blood dripping from the tines.

The stenciled name on the saddle skirt originally read, "MAJOR NEVILLE STRYKER." Weather and usage had worn letters off the leather, and people said what remained was more fitting– "EVIL STRYKER."

Stryker spent time between jobs in Pescadero. His daily routine included riding the three-mile trail to the beach and back. Upon intersecting the trail that ran above the beach bluff, he chose to ride up or down the beach. That was the most difficult decision he made each day while resting in the small California town. His work was demanding. He performed secret missions for Senator George Hearst. The missions often required discretion and Stryker's unique skills. He was proficient with a gun and blade. Most of his adversaries occupied graves. They did not convalesce; they decomposed.

One of the combatant sea lions waddled toward the ocean, conceding the females were not worth the ass-kicking. He slipped into the water to hunt fish instead.

A slight breeze blew in from the sea and brought with it the smell of kelp beds. With the fight show over, Stryker swung the roan's reins to head north along the bluff trail that he had ridden many times. The trail meandered among ice plants with daisies and sunflowers thrown in to add color, an easy ride. The roan knew the routine and Stryker let the horse keep its pace. He even allowed it to occasionally stop and munch on saltgrass. The roan once had a name, but Stryker never knew it. As with a lot of people he had met, he never paid much heed to remembering their names.

Years ago, Stryker had a wife. A pretty young thing with blonde hair and bright blue eyes; she was educated, well-connected, and she adored him. He felt the same about Leigh. That was her name, Leigh Enderson. He had left the Army then. She helped him get a job with J.P. Morgan as an investment banker in the House of Morgan. He specialized in munition companies. It was during an artillery firepower demonstration that Leigh lost her life. A shell landed out of the safety sector, killing Leigh and her family. Two men were to blame. One was a munitions competitor who switched the firing coordinates Stryker gave to the Howitzer's initial adjustment round. Stryker found the man and ran a saber through his liver. That earned him a "Wanted for Murder" poster. The likeness on the poster is not accurate. It showed him younger, clean-shaven, and handsome. The second man responsible for his wife's death now sits astride the roan. Stryker should have checked the coordinates for that first round. He could not shake the guilt. It wore on him like a heavy overcoat and recurring nightmares of Leigh's death would not allow the memories to fade. Maybe he didn't want them to. It was the only connection he had left with her, but the horrible dreams reminded him of his hand in her death, and he figured he deserved the damn things.

After Leigh's death, whenever he struck up an association with a woman, she ended up dead. A jinx. He knew it didn't make sense. Stryker was not a man given to the mystical. Nevertheless, it happened time after time. Like Pavlov's dog, Stryker had been conditioned, and he reacted to the curse. It was the reason he spent so much time in Pescadero. There was a woman in San Francisco he wanted desperately to stay alive. While riding the roan horse by the sea that morning, he thought about her.

Morgan Bickford was her name; she was a mining engineer and a widow. She worked for Senator George Hearst. Morgan was an attractive woman, widowed by a gang of Marxist thugs in a town called Egalitaria. Bickford was the town's previous name. Morgan and her husband owned a large ranch and a productive gold mine before the town was taken over by the ruthless politicos and renamed. They also murdered Morgan's husband. She had hired Stryker to get her property back. Since then, the two have maintained a close but limited relationship—limited because of the jinx. She was good-looking all right, and she felt damn good under him. However, it is the woman's principles and her philosophy that bound her to him. She stood for something he had not known before–reason. The irrefutable right that a man can keep what he earns, not have it taken and gifted to another. Stryker especially wanted to keep Morgan alive so that her ideals would not die with her.

Stryker was not a good man. Many saw him as a ruthless killer. Because of those fine qualities, Morgan introduced him to George Hearst. Hearst employed Stryker to procure the deed to the *San Francisco Examiner*, a newspaper the senator had won in a poker game. The uncooperative owner was reluctant to relinquish ownership. It was to be turned over to William Randolph Hearst, George's son. Stryker secured the deed, and Hearst paid him one hundred thousand dollars. The recalcitrant newspaper owner did not survive the transaction.

Morning mist gave way to a bright, sunny day. Only two bite-size white puffy clouds floated aloft in the blue. Stryker angled the roan up the hill from the sea to a big leaf maple tree. He swung from the saddle and pulled the canteen off the saddle horn. After stretching his legs, he took a swallow of the water. The canteen's canvas cover kept the water cool for him. He led the horse to a spring bubbling up through the crown of lush green grass. Stryker let the roan suck some water before leading it back to the shade tree. He leaned against the tree trunk while the roan munched on grass. Out in the Pacific, a steamship, looking like a toy boat, came into view. It appeared from the north, probably from San Francisco, and inched south. It might stop in Santa Cruz. Standing on the Santa Cruz pier a year ago is where he first realized Morgan still lived. He thought she died from a gunshot wound, and that the jinx got her. Stryker only sampled Morgan's charms on occasion, and she had survived.

Stryker lived in San Francisco, near the Embarcadero, until he was fourteen. Orphaned years earlier by union ruffians who had killed his parents, his uncle raised him. That is until he rammed the sai down the throats of two older boys who took delight in beating the shit out of him. On separate rainy nights, Stryker got each boy down in an alley and ended the beatings. Afterward, his uncle sent him east. It probably saved his life, but he got caught up in the Civil War. He fought for the North as a crewman on a Parrott Rifle. He saw the *pleasantries* of brutal combat up close and was recommended to West Point when the war ended.

It was time to ride back to Pescadero. Elena, who owned the boarding house where Stryker stayed in town, would have steak and eggs waiting for him. How she knew when he would return from the rides, he never knew. He never asked her. She was in her midfifties and a mixed breed like Stryker. A good woman, Elena cooked for him, did his laundry, and gave him an occasional massage. Nothing more. He paid her well.

He swung onto the roan and headed down the hill. Once on the sea bluff trail going south, the roan quickened the pace. Stryker allowed it. The horse was headed for its oats. It had been three months since he had been in San Francisco. What that meant, he had to admit to himself, was it had been three months since he had seen the woman. Stryker never traveled to San Francisco unless requested. Three months' rest was plenty. The days had become boring, and Stryker was not a man who was comfortable sitting on his ass. The requests usually appeared in the personal section of the *San Francisco Examiner*, put in the paper by Morgan. For the last two and a half weeks, rather than reading other sections before the personals, Stryker turned to them first. There was nothing so far.

The horse knew food waited in town, and it turned east onto Pescadero Road without prompting. The road meandered past Pescadero Marsh on a slight upgrade, and the roan bobbed its head, working harder to maintain pace. By the time Stryker rode into town and into the stable, the horse glistened with sweat. Loren's Stable, where Stryker kept the roan, was at the west end of town near Elena's boarding house. He dismounted, walked the horse, and let it drink a couple of times in the water trough before leading it to the stable. There, Stryker pulled off the saddle and blanket and threw them over the stall wall. He replaced the bit and bridle with a halter and then cooled the roan down with a wet sponge. He spent another fifteen minutes grooming the animal, brushing off loose hair, and removing burrs and thistles from the mane and tail. After filling the water bucket and throwing grains and oats on the floor, Stryker left the stable and walked to Elena's.

She met him at the front door. Five feet, four inches tall, Elena carried a few extra pounds. Not very many, though, because she maintained a busy routine, cooking, cleaning, making beds, and laundry chores. Her hair was pulled back in a tight bun that had more gray than black these days. Her husband had been dead for nine years now, and Elena wore a worried brow and seldom cracked a grin. It had been a struggle since he died of a stroke. Nevertheless, she opened the door for Stryker with a broad smile. With her brightened features, Stryker noticed remnants of past attractiveness.

Townsfolk used to ask Elena about Stryker, being mostly nosy. Some said he was a wanted man, hiding out. They conjectured he was a murderer. He looked like a killer, they said. Elena replied honestly that she knew nothing about the man. She did invite the curious to come by and ask him themselves. None did. The.44 on his hip looked well-used.

When Stryker went into town to buy horse soap, clothing, or other necessities, he was treated with muted courtesy. He often bought ammunition for the.44 Colt Peacemaker and the.44 Winchester carbine, and perhaps that had something to do with keeping curious mouths shut. They could have rightly figured he used a lot of bullets, and they did not want them used in Pescadero.

"Got breakfast waitin,' Mister Stryker." It had been a year, and she still referred to him as "mister." She didn't know his first name yet. It could take another year or two before he told her. Even after helping

Stryker into a washtub when he was injured, and after the massages she gave him when he only wore a towel, she kept a personal distance. At a time early on, she had inquired if he had ever been married. He simply replied, "She's dead." Elena never asked about his wife again.

Elena had prepared a breakfast of steak, eggs, biscuits, and coffee, strong and black; the steak portion was smaller those days. The eggs were sunny side up. A copy of the *San Francisco Examiner* lay beside his plate, four days old now. It was better than the ten days it used to be, getting it from Santa Cruz. Southern Pacific Rail Line ran tracks up to Boulder Creek last year, cutting delivery times. Pescadero was not on a main thoroughfare. That would be a decade, or so, later. Timber harvesting was what drove the train service around the Big Basin, and the little mission town of Pescadero did not qualify for profitable lumber commerce without rails. So, four days to get a newspaper from San Francisco to Saratoga and then on stagecoach over the Santa Cruz Mountains was timely. Visitors riding the coach over the mountains found it a grueling fifty-mile trip taking over two days.

Stryker opened the newspaper to the *personals*. The fourth item down read, "To N.S. You are needed. M.B." It was the usual notice. Elena stood by the table watching Stryker read the paper. He glanced up at her, and her face revealed she had already seen the message.

"Leaving after breakfast, Mister Stryker?"

"Reckon so." Stryker cut into the fried steak.

"I'll fix the provisions."

Stryker never spoke of his work to Elena, and she never ventured to ask where he went when he rode out of Pescadero. He went into the mountains. That is all she knew. He would be gone for weeks, sometimes months. Often, when he returned, he did not look well, and sometimes, when she gave him a massage, she noticed more scars. The massages started when Stryker fell asleep at the table after eating part of his dinner, exhausted from a long, dangerous trip. She walked around the table and rubbed his neck and shoulders. He eventually recovered and sat upright, saying nothing. She continued for a few minutes and stopped. Neither spoke. After that, and on the occasion when Stryker looked as if he needed it, Elena would rub his neck and shoulders. It took a long time before she got up the nerve to unbutton his shirt for a rub down. She had told him she had ointment for sore muscles, and he released his grip on her hand.

Stryker finished breakfast and went to his room to pack an extra shirt, denims, socks, long johns, and shaving items in the saddlebag while Elena put biscuits, cured ham, a couple of pears, and coffee grounds in a knapsack. No words were exchanged when he walked out the door.

Elena never knew when Stryker would return, or if he would return. She only knew whatever he did while away was dangerous. The shape his body was in when he returned told her that.

CHAPTER TWO

The ride over the Santa Cruz Mountains usually took Stryker two days. He often spent a night in a way station, if not in use by the stage line. Sometimes, he slept in the Congress Springs Hotel in Saratoga. He might stop there if he had slept on the ground the night before and had cleaned up for the train ride to San Francisco. Often, time did not permit the extra night, and Stryker had only stayed at the hotel three times.

Recently, the county had rebuilt the Redwood City and San Gregorio Turnpike, and that morning, Stryker headed north on the toll road to try out that route. The road was a stage route from San Francisco, Woodside, and Redwood City to the coast. It turned due south at San Gregorio, extending on down to Pescadero. Stryker normally took the stage road from Pescadero to Saratoga because of the better stage stops and the option of resting in the Congress Springs Hotel. That morning, he wanted to try a new route over the Santa Cruz Mountains.

One might wonder why Stryker spent time between jobs in Pescadero since it was so difficult to get to. He chose its remoteness on purpose. Easier access to San Francisco might be too tempting to travel to the city more often. That might have awakened the damn jinx and killed Morgan. Silly, nonsensical paranoia, he knew it. Nevertheless, he could not ignore the trail of dead women who got too close to him. Yeah, he could take the chance, after all, it was a stupid notion. Another woman, he might do it, but not with Morgan. Not with her.

The seven-mile ride on the stage road up to San Gregorio was a mild start to Stryker's journey, nowhere near the steep inclines ahead over the mountains. The town of San Gregorio, named after Saint Gregory, was a boom town in the 1880s for the wealthy to fish, hunt, sea-bathe, and watch boat races. The San Gregorio House, a two-story hotel, was the place to stay for the posh crowd. Stryker only stopped there briefly for the roan to drink from the water trough. The mixed breed was not a member of the posh crowd. A stagecoach sat in front of the San Gregorio Hotel as two men heaved travel bags on top of the stage. Stryker saw no passengers and guessed they must be still inside the hotel.

Stryker rode another two miles north to Tunitas Creek Road, the stage road up to the ridgeline where it junctioned with Kings Mountain Road. That road took travelers over the Santa Cruz Mountains and on down to Woodside. From Woodside, the stage line continued to Redwood City and the Southern Pacific Rail Line for the ride into San Francisco.

There had been times when Stryker felt trapped in his life. Only "allowed" to see Morgan occasionally, he took on dangerous tasks for Hearst and never felt he would ever settle down to live a normal life. What would be a normal life for him? It was too late to become a family man. Then again, he was not cut out to be a father. Could he return to work in finance again? He had been a successful investment banker for the House of Morgan, bringing munitions companies to the stock exchange. Leigh's connections with J.P. Morgan got him the job. Regardless, with the wanted poster all over the eastern part of the country, he could not risk a higher profile than what he has now.

Senator Hearst knew the reason for the posters and had persuaded President Cleveland to offer Stryker a pardon. For reasons known only to Stryker, he turned it down. Why turn it down? It could have been because his dead wife, Leigh, got no pardon. She would always be dead, and Stryker played a part in her death. Sure, he killed the other man primarily responsible for the errant round killing her, but in his mind, the proffered pardon also extended to his failure to double-check the firing coordinates on the artillery Howitzer. How could he accept a pardon for that? No, he, Major Neville Stryker, would be forever guilty. There could be no forgiveness, not with his way of thinking, and a pardon by the president or anyone else would ring hollow. He turned down the presidential pardon, and another was never offered.

Early on, Tunitas Creek Road ran through plentiful open meadowed farmland, and as the road began a gentle climb, shrub oak, and berry bushes filled the open spaces. As the stage road steepened with more curves, tall sugar pines lined both sides of the road, growing tall and thick on the western slopes of the Santa Cruz Mountains. Stryker and the roan climbed to higher elevations where regal redwoods stretched to the sky and tickled the clouds. Dark clouds often gave up their rain, like that day. The higher he rode, the harder it rained. Rain poured down in heavy sheets. The road wound sharply with hairpin turns. The downpour and the tree canopy overhead made it almost dark as night, and it was difficult to see the road ahead.

After seven miles of steady climbing, Stryker reined in the roan. He swung from the horse and led it to a creek with moss growth along the clear mountain runoff. As the roan sucked water, Stryker walked twenty feet upstream, took off the Stetson, and knelt to drink. The water was cold and sweet. He dunked his face in the stream and rested his haunches on his heels. With water dripping from his face, he surveyed his surroundings. Stryker spotted a doe, moving quietly to hide behind bushes a hundred yards up the hill.

A shout came from a male and higher up the mountain. Stryker took shallow breaths through his mouth to listen. He heard it again, sounding more distinct, more urgent.

He got to his feet, walked down to the roan, and led it back on the road. Stryker did not mount. Instead, he led the horse up the road and stopped every few minutes to listen. He heard nothing more until rounding a sharp turn, and then he heard more shouting and the crack of a whip, louder than before. It came from across a deep hollow the mountain road had to curve around. The hollow was over a quarter mile across, and it was a half mile on the road to skirt the depression. Trees and heavy foliage blocked his sight to see who was doing the shouting. Stryker stopped the roan and mounted. Finally, after looping around the hollow, the reason for the shouting and whip cracking came into view three hundred yards up the road.

A stagecoach leaned perilously over a steep embankment, a fifty-foot drop-off. Both wheels on its right side were stuck in a ditch caused by runoff rain from higher up. The wheels were sunk above the axles, and the carriage tilted at a perilous forty-five-degree angle. The coach being on an uphill grade didn't help. Attempting to get the coach back on the road, the driver swung the horses a sharp left, turning the front wheels away from the cliff. The right front wheel was at an angle, braking against an uphill pull and causing the coach frame to torque. *Could be worse,* Stryker thought. The driver could have snapped the wheel.

Two men dressed in brown tweed suits muddied above the knees, pulled mightily on a rope tied to the metal luggage rails atop the coach. Two women, wearing silk floral, ankle-length, dresses, held ineffective parasols against the rain, and stood on the other side of the road. A young girl stood between them. A coachman sat on the driver's bench, swearing loudly as he swung the whip.

When Stryker rode closer, he saw the other coachman in front of the horses, pulling hard on the harness and shouting encouragement to the team. He leaned back to near horizontal, fighting to maintain footing in the mud. That man and the little girl saw Stryker at the same time.

"Hold it, Clay," the front coachman shouted. He released the harness and pointed at the mixed breed coming up the road. The girl stared at Stryker, saying nothing.

"We could use a little help here, mister," Clay huffed, twisting his body around to address Stryker. He rested the whip hand on a knee and used a free hand to push his hat back. Sweat and rain poured off his face. "Me and Vance have been trying for the better part of two hours here."

Harnessed to the Concord stagecoach, the four draft horses huffed and snorted, their sides heaving mightily.

"It's been a long pull up the mountain and the horses are about to give out." Vance walked down past the horses to Stryker. "Passed another coach coming down the mountain. Pulled over, makin' room, and run in that hole." Vance hooked a thumb toward the stuck wheels. "The rain made it hard to spot. Rocked 'em back and forth but God-damn wheels sunk deeper." He turned to the women. "Sorry ma'ams," offering an apology for his cussing.

"Usually make a run up these mountains with six horses," Stryker allowed.

"We *wanted* to hold off for two more," Clay supplied. He did not sound happy about making the climb with only four horses.

"It's my fault, sir," one of the tweed suits spoke up, gripping the rope. He had to yell over the downpour. "I have an emergency in Woodside!"

"He's a doctor!" One of the women shouted.

Stryker matched her as the wife of the physician. She was the most attractive of the two women. He leaned forward, resting his forearms on the saddle horn.

"Might get out with five horses," Vance said to Stryker. He patted the roan's neck as he spoke.

"Ask him if he'll help," Stryker growled.

"Be worth twenty dollars to you, sir." The doctor dropped the rope and approached Stryker, who sat impassively on the roan.

"What?" Vance stepped back, looking puzzled.

"He does the pulling," Stryker deadpanned.

"Ask the horse, Vance," the doctor ordered. "I don't know your name, mister," he said to Stryker. "But a boy has sepsis in Woodside. I am the only specialist who can treat it in California. He's gonna die within twenty-four hours."

Stryker was unmoved.

"What's your horse's name?" Vance asked Stryker.

"Never knew it."

"Just ask the damn horse!" The doctor's wife screeched.

Vance moved in front of the roan, cupped its jowl, and stroked its muzzle. "Will you help us pull the stagecoach outta the mud?" Upon asking *nicely* and feeling visibly foolish, he looked up at Stryker, waiting for an answer. "Well?"

"You asked my horse."

"What did he tell you?" The doctor picked up on the ruse.

"Uh, well... I... he... He said he'd help!" Vance finally blurted.

Stryker swung off the roan.

"I'm Edward Feldman and this is my wife, Jessica," the doctor said, introducing himself and his wife. "Please call me Ed." Doctor Ed stood about five-foot-ten, fit, appearing intelligent, especially with the horned-rimmed glasses he wore. Not particularly handsome, but a doctor needn't be, to attract a good-looking woman.

Stryker tipped the Stetson with a forefinger.

"And these are my good friends from San Francisco, Earnest, his friend Eva, and her niece, Jilly."

Stryker offered another Stetson tip.

"Your name, sir?" Feldman extended his hand and then withdrew it when Stryker's hand remained by his side.

"Stryker." He began pulling off the roan's gear.

Vance came over to help. Vance pulled the saddle from the roan and lifted it to Clay, who secured it on top of the stagecoach. Stryker tossed the bit and bridle up to him as well, and then he moved away from the passengers to watch Vance lead the roan in front of the coach.

The draught horses were heavier and stouter than the roan, but they had had a long pull up the mountain and expended a lot more energy trying to get the coach free. They appeared worn out by the looks of their heaving sides. Stryker figured they could rest a bit while Vance attached a spare harness on the roan. Once Vance added the roan to the draft horses, Stryker stationed himself at the head of the re-arranged team and grasped the lead horse's bridle. "Keep the whip off my horse," he barked at Clay.

"All right everybody," Vance called out. "His horse told me if he's gonna help, we all have to help." Vance winked at Stryker. "We only have one shot at this. Women get behind the stage to push. Doc, you, and Earnest get on the rear wheels. I'll man a front one."

Jessica started to protest, but her doctor-husband shut her down. "Jess, we need to get to Woodside. Get behind the coach."

That elevated the physician a couple of notches for Stryker. He braced his boots in the mud and readied himself to pull.

"Everybody set?" Clay shouted.

"Yeah!" Everyone including Stryker yelled, "Yes!"

Clay then called, "Git up!" And he cracked the whip over the horses.

The coach lurched forward six inches and stalled. Clay yelled, "All on the whip, now!" He cracked it again. Stryker pulled on the harness; the men on the wheels pushed and grunted. The women pushed and grunted, too. The front right wheel lurched up against the lip of the ditch. It held there for a moment, and Clay cracked the whip again. "Push hard! Do it now!" Clay sounded frantic. The wheel lifted out, and he yelled, "Haw!" The horses strained to the left and the coach sprung forward, allowing the right rear wheel to lurch from the ditch as well. Clay had the horses pull twenty feet up the road and called out," Whoa, there!"

There were casualties–not bloody, not injurious, but muddy. Stryker remained on his feet with mud up to his knees. Vance and Doctor Feldman had slipped and fell. Earnest stayed upright, wading through the sinkhole with mud up to his waist. The women got the worst of it. When the coach lurched out of the hole, they fell face-first in the mud.

Husbands did their best to clean them off and not laugh. Clay and Vance also tried to help. Doctor Feldman and Ernest shooed them away. They didn't need help to clean the women's breasts. The only persons totally mud-free were Clay and Jilly, but the pouring rain soaked everybody. Upon getting some of the mud cleaned off with help from the rain, the women climbed back into the coach.

Stryker had remained by the roan. He had not offered to clean the women. He eyed Vance as he approached him, knowing what he was going to ask.

"Say, mister," Vance said. "It's only 'bout another mile and a half to the crest. Be interested in keeping your horse in harness until we get there, for a full thirty dollars. We swap out the horses there at Grab Town. I think your horse will be okay with it."

"Make it fifty," Fellman added, joining them. "Please, mister, it's important not to have more delays," the doctor said. "If you want more, I'll pay."

"The coach carries six people comfortably, eight pinched together," Vance interrupted.

Stryker momentarily weighed asking for two hundred, then said, "Thirty's fine." He climbed in the coach last. The two women, Eva and Jessica sat with Doctor Feldman, facing forward on the padded leather seats. Ernest and Jilly were opposite them facing rearward. Stryker took the open seat next to Ernest.

"Everyone situated in there?" Clay called from the driver's bench.

"All set," Feldman yelled back.

With the crack of the whip and a shout at the horses, the stagecoach lurched forward. The Concord's interior was plush. The cushions were tan padded leather with embossed red leather on the walls, which matched the red exterior of the stagecoach. The Concord stagecoach was the best of the day. It had leather straps for springs called thoroughbraces for passenger comfort. The straps also provided a lighter load than the metal springs used for city trips. The coach swayed back and forth as it lurched up the hill, and the passengers swayed along with it.

Eva closed her eyes and gently swayed with the coach. Feldman studied a leather-bound book he had pulled from his carry bag. Ernest rode silently along, idly staring at nothing. Jilly rested her head on her uncle's shoulder. Jessica stared at Stryker with not-too-approving eyes.

"What kind of work do you do, Mister Stryker?" Mrs. Feldman finally asked. Her question dripped with sarcasm.

"Odd jobs."

"Ed and Ernest went to Harvard together. That is how we all know each other." Jessica smiled politely.

Stryker nodded. *I think I can keep from slapping the woman for a mile and a half.*

"Ernest writes for the *San Francisco Examiner*. He earned his degree in philosophy," Eva awoke and added. "He and William Randolph Hearst worked on the Harvard Lampoon together." Eva smiled politely. "Have you ever read that paper, Mister Stryker?"

"On occasion."

"Oh, you have?" Jessica seemed genuinely surprised Stryker could read.

Stryker's pale eyes grew icier.

"Where did you go to school, Mister Stryker?" Eva asked.

Doctor Feldman sensed the women were inviting trouble, and he tried to move the talk away from schooling. "Ernest just authored a well-received poem for the paper. Tell 'em about it, Ernest."

Ernest, hardly the boastful type, did go on to describe the poem. "It's called *Casey at the Bat*, a rather humorous take on big-headed heroes." He turned to Stryker. "I'm surprised it has done so well, actually."

"William owns the newspaper. We are all good friends with him. Not so much with his father, George, though."

"George Hearst," Stryker said.

"Yes, but of course, I don't think you would know him," Jessica snipped. "He is a United States senator." The woman did not know that Stryker, while working for George, killed the man who previously owned *The Examiner* and got it handed over to William Randolph. He killed several during the effort[1].

Stryker said nothing.

"Did you read the poem by Ernest?" Eva asked, smiling politely.

"No."

"But you do read the paper on occasion," Jessica scoffed.

"West Point," Stryker said.

"What about West Point?" Jessica asked, a puzzled look on her face.

---

1. *Payback Is Hell- Book III in the Evil Stryker Series*

"My schooling."

"You went to West Point?" Edward asked. His interest piqued.

Stryker nodded.

"Were you in the war?" The doctor was now engaged.

Before Stryker could reply, Jessica interjected, "What tools of trade do you use now?" The woman could not stop with the snide comments.

"Guns," Stryker said. Then to Ed, "In the war, yes." He looked at Jessica, "And on occasion… a razor."

That rendered Jessica and everyone else in the coach stiffer, except Jilly, who had fallen asleep, with much to ponder. The conversation lagged after that.

"Stop the stage!" The gruff command came from outside the stagecoach. Then there was a gunshot and a groan from one of the guards.

"Good God!" Ernest exclaimed. "It's a hold-up!"

"Everyone outta' the stage," said the same gruff male.

"Ladies first," Stryker growled, and he pulled the Peacemaker.

"You're one of them!" Jessica flashed hateful eyes at the mixed breed.

"You, first. Get out," Stryker ordered her.

"Mister Stryker…" Feldman lost his nerve, and he could only shake his head.

Stryker cocked the Colt.

Jessica scooted from the padded bench and moved hunched over past Eva to grip the door handle. She opened the coach door and peered out. Looking back at her husband, she whispered, "Three of them." She edged closer to the opening and turned back to Stryker. After telling him, "You bastard!" she faced frontward and placed her foot on the step pad.

Stryker looked out the window and spotted the three robbers standing by the stagecoach. Two men had their pistols pointed at Jessica. The third man had his revolver trained on Clay and Vance. Only one of them, if the shot driver was dead.

Stryker lurched from his seat and booted Jessica's rump. Flying from the coach, she shrieked and landed face down on the road. The three robbers focused on the attractive screamer who was lying in the mud.

Stryker dove out the stage firing the Peacemaker and got off two shots before landing on Jessica's back. The first.44 round smashed in the chest of the closest robber, and the second bullet gut-shot the man next to him. The third robber took off running. Stryker settled himself on Jessica, rose on his elbows, and took aim. He fired two more bullets, and the second round brought him down.

"Ga, ah…" But Jessica couldn't get the words out. Stryker had knocked the wind out of her. He pushed off, and she rolled over, gasping for air.

Stryker pinched Jessica's nose, inhaled deeply, then pressed his mouth on hers and blew. She fought hard to push him off, but he took another deep breath and blew air into her mouth again. Then he sat back and waited. She began to catch her breath, and Stryker got to his feet. He swung the Colt's barrel around, checking for more robbers. Seeing none, he holstered the gun.

Jessica struggled to her feet with no help from Stryker. The front of her floral dress was plastered with mud. She stood and watched him walk over to the robber with a bullet in his belly.

The robber sat cross-legged, holding his stomach. He lifted his head when Stryker stopped in front of him. "I need a doctor." He, like the other two thieves, had yet to reach twenty years of age.

Stryker drew the Colt, pointed it at the young man's forehead, and fired. The big.44 round blasted a chunk of brain through an inch-wide hole out the back of his skull. None of the robbers would make it out of their teens. Young and inexperienced, they had heard the stagecoach was easy pickings on top of the mountain. It might have been, had they not run into the mixed breed. The other two robbers were already dead when Stryker got to them.

Clay and Vance remained seated on the driver's bench. Clay had taken the bullet. He sat slumped against Vance, who finally lowered his arms as Stryker came around the front of the stage.

"They shot Clay," Vance said to Stryker. "Got him in the shoulder,

I think." He reached for the wounded man, pushed him back against the cargo rack, and unbuttoned his shirt.

"I'll be all right," Clay mumbled. The red blotch was growing bigger around the bullet hole in Clay's shirt.

"I'll get the doctor," Stryker said, turning back toward the Concord's open door.

"Jessica!" Doctor Feldman shouted. He leaped from the coach, missed the step pad, and crashed into his wife. She fell in the mud again, this time on her butt.

"Thank you, Ed." Jessica rolled to her knees.

"I'm sorry, dear." The good doctor reached for his wife's arm, but she got to her feet without his help.

"You and Eva may want to change clothes while they swap horses in Grab Town," Feldman offered dryly. He stifled a laugh.

"Clay's got a bullet in him," Stryker said, rescuing the doctor.

Doctor Feldman treated Clay's gunshot wound and used bandages and alcohol he carried in his medical bag. The bullet missed bone and exited out the back of his shoulder. There was no need to dig out lead. Feldman made a sling out of Clay's bandanna and agreed it was okay for him to remain up front with Vance. Clay climbed onto the driver's bench, using his good arm, and he rested the shotgun across his knees.

"We oughta bury 'em," Vance suggested.

"We're in a hurry," Stryker grunted.

No one argued.

The passengers piled into the coach and took the same seats they had before the stop.

The Concord jostled up the hill for a full ten minutes before Eva broke the silence. "I wish the rain would stop," she said, eyeing her husband and arching her eyebrows as if to encourage conversation.

"Hmmm, yes," Ernest offered, nervously tapping his foot. "Perhaps it will before long."

"Please stop tapping your foot, Ernest. You do that and it drives me crazy."

"It's a short drive, my dear." Ernest stopped the tapping. His nerves were a bit frayed. The poet had not realized he was foot-tapping. He would not have wanted to aggravate the man sitting next to him, especially since the mixed breed was the reason for the frayed nerves. Ernest thought about exchanging seats with his niece.

"And getting shorter," was Eva's retort.

Ernest halted the *short drive* with his wife. Her fuse was close to being lit. He withdrew a notebook from his leather case and scribbled. None of the words rhymed.

Jessica acted lost in her thoughts, ignoring the *Bickersons,* and kept her eyes trained on Stryker who was reading *The Examiner*. Ernest had not objected when Stryker picked it up during the bickering.

Stryker knew Jessica was staring at him, and he disregarded her while he kept reading the paper.

Jessica's ruminations swirled in a silent soliloquy:

Look at him. Reading the paper as if nothing had happened. He just killed three men. Boys, for God's sake! Only boys! If I had known he was going to kill them, I would've given them money or something. Tried to stop them, or better yet, stop him. He didn't need to kill them. That man across from me is nothing but a ruthless killer. Mean, ugly, ruthless bastard. I hate men like him. Despise them. Killing is the only thing they know. He cannot have a wife. God, who could be with a man like that? He would beat her.

"I suppose we should thank you, Stryker," Doctor Feldman said. "Would have been more of a delay, and who knows, someone else could have been shot." Feldman waited expectantly for Stryker to acknowledge his words of gratitude. It never came.

Stryker continued reading the paper, and the good doctor dropped the gratitude effort.

Jessica continued her silent soliloquy: *My husband, always the gentleman. Polite man, refined, not like that brute across from me. Edward saves lives. Stryker takes them. No remorse. Why does God allow men like him to be on earth? He is a killer. That is what his odd jobs are, killing people. I cannot understand why men must be like him. Why can't they all be like Edward? Good men.*

Jessica glanced sideways at her husband with a feint, but heartfelt, smile. Then returned her gaze to Stryker. Her expression hardened.

Not like him. Even though he saved us, I guess that is what he did, saved us. I don't think he had to kill them. All of them, anyway. Certainly not that last boy. Edward could have kept that boy alive, and he might have turned out to be a better person. It happens. Sometimes things happen and it changes a life around. But no. Stryker aimed his damn gun at the boy's head, ignored his pleading, and shot him. I will never forget the young man's eyes. Ruthless bastard, Stryker. I hate him. I hope someone kills him just like that. The same way. And I hope he pleads for his life.

A corner of Jessica's mouth twitched at the thought.

Yes, I would like to see him beg. Wonder who else has begged for his life and Stryker killed them. Men? Good men? God, I hope not. Women? Oh, Jesus Lord. Has he killed women, too? My God, he probably has. If they crossed him, I could see him doing it.

Jessica's imagination was running wild, taking her to places she would never have thought about going, nevertheless, she drifted along with it.

I guess some women would take up with the likes of him. Crazy ones, at least. Don't know any better. I cannot imagine anyone going to bed with him. They would have to be insane, for sure. They could not possibly get pleasure from someone like him. Just look at him. Sitting there reading the paper. He scares me. He would surely scare any woman. Why would they sleep with him? Does he rape 'em? Maybe not. There are women out there who like that sort of thing, that kind of man, I suppose. I have known them. They even seemed like normal women, but when they talked..., they talked about sleeping with someone like Stryker, and having sex with him. Jesus! They seemed sincere. I did not believe them, though. What in God's name did he do to make them want to do it with him? One said nothing. Ralene, yes, it was Ralene. She said she liked it. Liked it? Oh, my God. She said he took her long and hard. Still thinks about it she told me. I imagine he took her, pleased himself, and left. But no. She said it was the best she'd ever had. Did things to her she never knew about. I do not believe her. Edward does things with me, politely, and gentlemanly. My husband is a refined, cultured, gentleman. Ha, certainly not like the man who did it with Ralene. That look on her face when she remembered, though. Big, dreamy smile, and dancing eyes, and she had hummed to herself as she walked away. Did it with that man while she was married to another, she told me. She's still married, as far as I know. Happily, she claims. She said she never saw that other man again. A tall thin man, with long black hair, and a week-old beard. Had pale gray eyes. Pale gray eyes? Wait! Holy Mother of God! Oh no! It could not be. But maybe, just maybe, it was Stryker!

Jessica squinted hard at Stryker. He looked up at her. She froze.

Was it him? Oh, my goodness! He's looking straight at me like he knows. No, he couldn't know, could he? Jessica felt a twinge inside, deep down. Very deep down. She gave Stryker an alluring smile. He nodded, dipping the Stetson in return.

It is unlikely Stryker is the man who spawned a sparkle in her friend, Ralene's, eye. One never knows, though. Not all the mixed breed's exploits are recounted on these pages.

That night, after Doctor Feldman completed the life-saving procedure with the young sepsis patient, he arrived home late. Jessica dragged him into bed, and made passionate love to him, doing things she had only heard about, and the good doctor wondered what in the world had gotten into his wife.

CHAPTER THREE

"Coming into Grab Town!" Vance shouted from atop the stage. Grab Town was once a tiny sawmill community. Loggers cut and milled logs for transport by wagon to Redwood City's loading docks. No property rights existed. A person just "grabbed on" to property when another left it. There was nothing there now except a stable used by the stage line for swapping horses. No townsfolk greeted the travelers, just two men and a six-horse team to bring the stagecoach down the mountain.

Jilly jumped from the coach and yelled, "We got robbed!"

"Robbed, huh?" One of the stagemen grunted while holding the new team. "Second time this week."

Eva and Jessica followed Jilly out of the coach, trying to brush off the mud that had begun to cake on their dresses. Then Ernest followed, who corrected Jilly. "Three of them, but they didn't rob us."

Stryker was the last person to get off the stagecoach.

"They tried," Vance said, climbing back on top of the coach for Stryker's saddle. "Got shot, by him." He nodded toward Stryker as he picked up the saddle. "Someone take this," Vance called to the two station men as he leaned over the luggage rails with the saddle and gear. One man jumped forward and held up his arms for the gear.

"You need a hand, Clay?" The other man asked, seeing Clay edge off the driver's bench, preparing to climb down with one good arm.

"Hell no, dammit." Clay swung off the coach and hit the ground hard, stumbling when he landed but staying on his feet. "One of 'em winged me, or I would've shot 'em." Clay was acting a little grouchy. During the rest of the ride to what remained of Grab Town, he had time to think about his role in the robbery affair. Being the stagecoach guard, he was attempting to save face.

"We're in a hurry," Vance called out, climbing down from the coach. "Got a sick boy in Woodside and the doctor here needs to get there to save his life." He pointed a finger at Doctor Feldman who added, "It's urgent we get there as soon as possible."

Stryker pulled the harness and straps off the roan as fast as he could. He wanted to get on the road ahead of the stagecoach, and not let it catch up. One of the station men helped Stryker while his partner brought up the new horse team.

"You shot 'em, mister?" The station hand with a rubicund complexion talked as he worked on the horse team's harness, pulling off the collars, bridles, traces, and straps. Since Stryker failed to acknowledge his initial query, he tried again. "Must be pretty good with a gun."

Stryker stripped the harness gear off the roan without answering. He put a bridle on the horse and led it to the saddle, which was lying by the stage. He could hear the station men talking low and figured they were discussing him. A couple of glances cast his way confirmed it. He threw on the saddle, cinched it, brought the reins over the roan's ears, booted the stirrup, and swung into the saddle. Once settled on the roan, Stryker pulled the reins about and headed back onto Tunitas Creek Road. He traveled along the ridgetop for a little over two miles to Kings Mountain Road and then turned the roan to go down the twisting six miles to Woodside.

A new job for Hearst. A secret mission. Will probably require Stryker's unique skills. Not as in a speaking engagement. No. Few words were needed on those jobs. He did not dwell on what the senator might have for him. He would find out soon enough. Stryker's mind was on something else. The roan kept a good pace as if it knew the road, and Stryker let the reins hang loosely in his hand. That something else was the female mining engineer who worked for Hearst. A couple of times, he had thought she might have died: once in Egalitaria and again when kidnapped and held for ransom. Both times, he figured the jinx took her, but that was not to be. A woman like Morgan does not come along often, maybe only once. An attractive intellectual female with strong philosophical views. She taught him how to use reason as a moral compass, concepts he had not thought about before. The fruits of a man's labor belong to him, to do with as he sees fit, whether he uses his earned wealth to enhance life's comforts, exchanges it in fair trade, or uses it for investment, it is his to do with as he pleases, which includes charity if he chooses. Earned wealth, Morgan stated often, is not the province of government. It does not belong to bureaucrats for redistribution. Redistribution, progressive, fair share, social transfer payment, these are euphemisms, she had said. They hide what those innocent-sounding words and phrases really mean– INSTITUTIONALIZED THEFT. Once Stryker heard Morgan's reasoning, he agreed with it. He relished the times they had together, especially when she expounded on her socio-philosophical viewpoints. To him, they rang true and clean. Yes, he enjoyed the physical, the sex, but it was the woman's mind that made her so desirable. "What did he do *right* to deserve her?" Stryker ruefully asked of himself, riding the roan down the road. "Shit, what did she do *wrong* to deserve me?" He got a little twitch at the corner of his mouth. Regardless, he looked forward to seeing her again.

Winding down the eastern slope of the Santa Cruz Mountains, not as many redwoods grew along Kings Mountain Road due to the cutting, but there were still plenty of Douglas fir, tan oak, and maple trees to shade the trail on which Stryker rode. There were various berry bushes and mountain laurels as ground cover. Sometimes, when the road made a wide switchback, he could hear the stagecoach traveling behind him. Vance and Clay's voices and the stage's rolling racket carried across the open spaces. When they seemed too close behind him, he spurred the roan into a quicker pace. Those people on the stage were not particularly annoying. Nonetheless, Stryker preferred his own thoughts as he rode and did not want them interrupted. It took about an hour and twenty minutes to reach Woodside. He stopped briefly to rest and water the roan at a horse trough on the east side of town before riding on to Redwood City, where deforestation had eliminated almost all the redwood trees. The town got the name for its lumber milling business.

Redwood City, a port city on the San Francisco Bay, is the oldest city on the peninsula, established in 1850, and had a population of around 1,500 when Stryker rode into town. Shipbuilding, in addition to lumber milling, was the two main commercial enterprises. Being a port town, it had its share of saloons and bordellos. Stryker was more interested in dinner and the roan's care than he was in liquor and entertainment. He continued down Broadway Street to the livery and paid a boy $1.50 to feed, water, and wash down the animal while he went about finding someplace to eat dinner. The next train for the city left two hours later at 8:10 PM.

He found Laura's Kitchen down Main Street where Broadway and Main intersected. The place was crowded, suggesting Laura was a good cook. It was a small bistro with seven linen-covered tables. It had a white wainscot with the top half painted turquoise on the walls. Green and white checkered tiles covered the floor. Open windows on both side walls provided light, and a light breeze blew through the openings, rustling the white linen curtains. Exceptionally clean, it had a spacious serving window in the back wall between the dining room and the kitchen area. The swinging door led to the kitchen. A table busser cleaned a two-person table in the far corner, and Stryker headed for it at the same time as another man.

"I've been waiting a half-hour," the well-dressed, not-quite-overweight fellow in a gray suit, said. He quickly sized up Stryker. "However, I would be willing to share the table with you."

Stryker and the stranger pulled out chairs and sat. Neither broke the silence while they each read their menus. It listed four chicken selections and three fish choices. Stryker flipped the single sheet over, looking for beef or pork listings, but the back page was empty.

His dining partner eyed the blank page as well. He had a ruddy face with enough age lines to indicate he was past forty. Looked fit enough, though. "I guess we're having chicken or fish tonight," he allowed in a droll monotone. "I'm new in Redwood City," he said placing the menu sheet on the table. "Is there another place to eat that might have real meat?" The fellow looked ready to bolt from the place.

"Passing through, myself." Stryker let the menu slip to the table.

A young waitress approached their table. "No beef or pork," Stryker said to her. It was another one of those interrogatives Stryker asked in a statement. Not sure why he did it, but it irritated folks at times. It was as if he asked with inflection to indicate a question, it would put him at a disadvantage. Who knew? It did put the recipient off balance, trying to figure out what the hell Stryker meant. Usually, it took them a stumble or two to gin up a reply.

"Uh, that's right, we have no beef or pork," the waitress replied. We don't have a good butcher in town. Maybe someday we will. "In the meantime, what would you like? The fried chicken and scallops are favorites." The girl was polite and easy on the eyes: trim, shapely, and attractive. It was possible a better meal could be found somewhere else, Stryker reasoned, but the girl's features could make food palatable. A surly male server someplace else could repress an appetite. "Fried chicken, mashed potatoes, green beans, and coffee."

"I'll have the same," the table partner said, as he handed the menu to the waitress. "Name's Tuite, Bud Tuite." He introduced himself, watching the waitress walk away. "Not bad." Then Tuite turned to Stryker. "Odd there is no meat butcher in town. Maybe they had one, and something happened to him."

"Stryker."

"How's that?" Tuite cocked his eyebrows.

"Stryker."

"Oh, your name!" Tuite had his arms crossed, resting on the table surface. He offered a handshake. Got it halfway across the table, and upon realizing the man across from him wasn't responding, he pulled his hand back. "I'm a meat cutter myself," he said, moving past an awkward moment. I could set up a shop here." Bud canted his head the way a person does when being pensive. He nodded thoughtfully. "Just need to get someplace to do it. I already have the tools and cutlery, the finest Gyuto knives from Japan." Tuite saw that Stryker was not impressed. "Know anything about knives, butchering meat, Stryker?" He broached a pleasant smile.

"Some."

"You've cut meat, too?" Tuite had eyed the.44. when he first saw Stryker may have suspected he was in another kind of work.

"At times."

"Well now," Tuite cleared his throat. He was starting to look a bit nervous. Stryker's brief replies had not been friendly. "You familiar with Japanese Gyuto knives? They are the best money can buy. I have a complete butchering and carving set. I bought them in Japan for thirty-six hundred US dollars and brought them to the United States. They are all I use to cut meat," Tuite boasted. "What kind of blades do you cut with, Mister Stryker?" He asked, sporting a cocky grin.

"Straight razor."

"Oh." The grin vanished. "Uh, here comes our chicken."

The conversation lagged while the two men ate the chicken breasts with their hands. Even though the fried chicken breasts were unusually large and could have been easily cut, Tuite did not use his knife. He finished his meal quickly and excused himself while Stryker sipped his second cup of coffee.

The owner, Laura, came out from the kitchen into the dining room, making the rounds to each table, and speaking with the guests. A fortyish, attractive woman, she approached Stryker's table with a broad, friendly, smile, and the food bill. "Did you like your dinner?"

"Yes, liked the chicken."

Laura glanced at the empty chair and the finished food plate. "Your friend had to leave early?"

"Reckon so."

"Would you like an apple muffin with your coffee?" Laura swept an arm toward the kitchen counter where muffins were stacked on a platter.

"No thanks, got a train to catch." Stryker lifted his cup and drained the rest of the coffee.

"My husband, George fries the chicken. I make everything else." Laura said, unfazed by Stryker's menacing features. She then added, "I'll tell him you liked the chicken." She turned to leave.

"That man who was sitting here is a butcher." Stryker pointed the cup at the vacant chair. "Said he was a butcher. Might want to set up shop in town. Hear you need one. His name's Tuite."

"I will tell George that, too. Stop in again next time you're passing through. Might have steak for you." Laura spun and headed back to the kitchen.

Stryker stood, put three dollars on the table for a two-fifty meal, and walked from the restaurant. The sun sank behind the mountains and light was fading fast. He had over an hour wait for the San Francisco train. It was beginning to get loud with loggers and sailors whooping it up in the saloons. He had enough time to down a beer or two in one of them, but he never fit in with that crowd. He'd rather have a quiet beer someplace. Out of an old habit, his right hand hung close to the Peacemaker. He didn't expect trouble, but old habits died hard. Besides, it was not a bad one to have.

A slight breeze rustled the maple trees along the street as he made his way toward the livery. He could not see the leaves fluttering; he just heard them. The sidewalks had planks missing, and he stepped out onto the dirt street where the walking was smoother. In Laura's, he overheard that the town planned to pave the streets and the sidewalks next year. No use replacing the boards. Progress often takes a step backward before moving forward.

The idle thoughts rambled through Stryker's head as he strolled down the street, passing three saloons and loud drinkers within. The moon peaked out over the stable a couple of hundred yards ahead and cast a feint shadow behind him. Most of the people out were men going to or coming from saloons. The only females Stryker saw were "ladies of the evening" trolling in the streets. The lowest level of prostitutes, but at least they did not pay a bartender part of their earnings. They were not the most attractive women, though. Poor things, they were well past prime and not wanted in the saloons, so they remained outside where the light was dimmer. Their favorite targets were older drunks with spare change that jingled in their pockets. Easy money, but there was not much of it. The unappealing *ladies* were no temptation to Stryker, although he did feel a twinge of pity for their plight, but only a slight twinge.

A lantern hung outside the livery. The eight-foot-wide sliding door was shut, however, the latch door next to it hung open. Stryker slid it apart and stepped inside. There were no lit lanterns; it was very dark. He heard a movement in a stall to his left. Sounded as if someone moved about in the hay. Then he heard voices. A female, an older one. A male, a younger one. A streetwalker was educating the lad. It might even be his first lesson and for less than a dollar. *What the hell? Fair trade.* Stryker's eyes adjusted to the light, and he continued to the roan's stall. He talked a bit to the animal, which he seldom did, and a little louder than normal, pretending he was alone with his horse. He threw on the saddle and left two bits for the stable hand on a rail before leading the horse outside. All the while he continued to talk to the roan. The mixed breed could sometimes be considerate.

The San Francisco train had not yet arrived in Redwood City. Nevertheless, Stryker brought the roan to the station and hitched it to an outside rail. Once inside, he found out the train was on time, and he bought tickets for him and the horse. Most passengers had not arrived for the scheduled departure, and only a smattering of people sat on the wooden benches. He took a seat at the secluded end of one bench and picked up a crumpled copy of the *San Francisco Examiner*. Idly turning the pages, he came to a photograph of the Cliff House and Seal Rocks. He remembered when he had taken Morgan to dine there and walked on the beach below. If Stryker were predisposed to smile, he would have done so now, but he did not. It wasn't in the man. However, he made a mental note to take her there again soon. He laid the paper aside as more passengers drifted into the station. Among them, an elderly man and woman eyed him with suspicion, and they sat on the oak bench a good distance away from him.

Stylish, that is how the white-haired couple appeared. The

gentleman wore a straw fedora hat with a light blue ribbon band, a cream-colored blazer, white cotton slacks, a pale blue shirt, which superbly matched the hat band, and light sand-colored wing-tip oxfords. Sharp. The gentle lady was similarly dressed in the same colors, except she wore a pleated skirt, white stockings up to the calves, and fashionable reading glasses. The rest of her attire coordinated impeccably with the gentleman's, including the straw fedora. Stylish. The man had a newspaper under his arm with an umbrella. The woman carried a book, which could have been a diary. When she sat, she wrote in it. They sparred about fifteen words with one another while waiting for the train.

By the time the Southern Pacific pulled into the station, the room was crowded. With bench space taken, men stood to let women sit. Stryker went outside, pulled his saddlebags off the roan, and watched as it was walked up the wooded ramp into the stock car. Then, aiming to procure his preferred rear seat on the train, he worked his way to the second coach. Without being more pushy than normal, which was always damn rude, he managed to move near the front of the waiting passengers and hopped aboard to shove his way to the rear seat. With his back against the wall, he faced forward. All the seats were padded with red velvet cushions, a pleasant respite for his butt after a long ride in the saddle. He picked up the paper to read while the other passengers filed in. Naturally, the seat next to him remained empty, as did the two seats across from him, facing rearward. That was until the elderly well-dressed couple made their way down the aisle. They were unable to find a seat except for the one across from the menacing man in the back. They appeared uncomfortable, especially the woman who seemed nervous.

The train lurched forward just as night had arrived. Lights passed outside the window like fireflies. California has lightning bugs in the south, although it's not a huge population. Only the females glow faintly on the ground.

Two train stops later, the woman spoke first. Perhaps she noticed Stryker perusing through the financial section of *The Examiner* and decided he might not shoot them. It was when Stryker glanced up and caught her staring at him that she spoke.

"My husband, Barclay, worked on the London Stock Exchange," she said.

Stryker laid the paper aside. Five long minutes passed with the two of them staring at one another. She waited for him, and he debated if he wanted to engage in a conversation. Her mention of the stock exchange and her accent clued Stryker that she was British. That explained the natty attire. *All right.* "Good for him," he said.

"He's retired now."

Stryker nodded.

By this time, the woman guessed she would have to carry the conversation. "Worked there fifty-two years. Retired six years ago."

Stryker lowered the Stetson brim, stretched out his legs, and then crossed them.

"You have an interest in the stock market, sir?" the elderly man asked.

A forefinger pushed up the hat brim. Stryker studied the old man's face. He saw an honest, unpretentious gaze. "Not any longer."

"You lost money?"

"No."

"Good, the market went through a rough patch for a while." The smile on Barclay seemed genuine. "As my wife, Audrey, said, I am retired now, but I still study the stock market. Old habit, I guess."

Stryker peered out the train window and only saw his reflection. He was tempted to talk with the man in the glass. Instead, he swung back to Barclay. "Old habits."

"Me and Audrey moved back to Scottland, my childhood home after retirement. Could not stay, though."

Stryker lifted his hand to lower the Stetson, but Barclay quickly added, "They'd turned Tobermory into a Socialist hellhole."

Stryker dropped his hand.

The three of them stared at one another for a minute. Train wheels clacked a monotonous cadence.

Although Stryker held his tongue, he gave his full attention to Barclay, as if encouraging the old man to continue.

"Miserable place now. Used to be like a fairytale you would see in a book, a small idyllic fishing village. Not anymore." Barclay paused again.

"Go on."

"Have you heard of this new Marxist movement?"

"Hate it."

Barclay figured he was on firm ground with the man across from him. "Abomination is what it is. A scourge, a plague on mankind. They came to Tobermory, espousing a new government without government. New men, organizers of the new way. I suppose, at first, it seemed an appealing, alternative relief from the monarchies. I might have thought so myself." Barclay glanced at his wife who nodded in agreement.

"Everything would be equally owned. No king would rule, and no taxes paid. In return, though, everything, I mean everything, had to be equally shared. Shop sales, even the shops themselves, and eventually homes and private possessions. Men stopped working. Why work if everything earned is taken and re-distributed? Then, the word got out that not everything was shared equally. The new leaders kept more and more for themselves. Audrey and I left before the violence started." Barclay put an arm around his wife. "Ever hear of such a thing Mister…?"

"Stryker. Yes, I have."

"Your town?"

"Not my town. I was passing through. A town called Bickford. Everything in it turned to shit."

"Uh, I see. The same thing happened?"

"Yes."

Is it still like that, Stryker?"

"No."

"What happened to change it?"

"The Marxists died off."

"A sickness?"

"I killed 'em."

Barclay turned to his wife, and they exchanged glances.

"Stryker, would you like to visit Tobermory?"

Barclay got no reply.

Barclay and Audrey did not speak to Stryker again until they stopped in Burlingame. Once boarding passengers settled in their seats, and the train pulled out of the station, Barclay asked, "Sir, if you don't mind my inquiry, do you have a profession?"

"Odd jobs," Stryker replied. He lowered the Stetson. He figured their next question might be if he were for hire. However, it never came, and no more conversation took place between them until the Southern Pacific pulled into San Francisco.

The thunderous engine came to a rest inside the Ferry House, and belched thunderous steam blasts, as though catching its breath after the long haul. The sound of the engine's puffy coughs reverberated off the wooden walls of the station, rattling the glass windows in the cars. The racket added urgency for passengers to hurry off the train and get out of the noisy building.

"It was a pleasure meeting you, Mister Stryker," Audrey shouted as she and Barclay stood by their seats. Barclay picked up their two carry bags. Audrey extended her hand to Stryker and quickly withdrew it.

Being a former officer and a gentleman, Stryker allowed the two stylish Britons to walk off the train ahead of him. Admittedly, he was no longer an officer, and he never was a gentleman. Barclay hustled his wife to walk ahead of him down the aisle.

Stryker stepped from the train carrying the saddlebag and walked back to the livestock car to get the roan. A livestock handler walked it down the ramp. Stryker ran a hand down the roan's legs, checking for injuries or soreness. After finding none, he paid the Ferry House hostler two dollars to stable it with feed and water. Few people were in the Ferry House[1] that night. All the shops except one were closed for the night. Only night workers, security men, and late travelers were in the building, all moving about and not talking. None of them paid

---

1. The Ferry House, a wooden building, was replaced with a reinforced, steel-framed, arched structure in 1898 and renamed the Ferry Building

Stryker any attention. A newspaper stand that also served coffee was still open. He bought a cup of the brew and waited near a window for the Market Street cable car to carry him to the Palace Hotel.

Peering through the glass, Stryker thought about how San Francisco had changed over the last thirty years. That is how long it had been since he was a boy there. Changes, new brick buildings, tall ones now, new shops, new businesses, bigger crowds, more men in suits, more bustles on women's asses. When he returned from the east, he hardly recognized the city. All his folks were gone or dead. He had changed too. When he shaved, the man in the mirror was a stranger with the lines, the wrinkles, yes, wrinkles, but it was more than that. It was like something got wrung out of him. Wars, fighting in them, do something to the insides of a man. You don't look at people the same way. They don't see you the same way either.

Stryker sipped the coffee. It was stale but hot, and he had to take small sips. That was all right. He figured it must have come from the bottom of the pot, though. The coffee grounds in it were an indication. That was all right, too. He had strained camp coffee through his teeth lots of times, so what? It started to rain. It hit the window, making little rivulets streaking down the glass, making it tougher to see outside.

He was fifteen when he went into the Army for the North. Almost twenty when the war ended. Five long years that seemed like ten. A year in the Army is a long time. A year of fighting in it is even longer. In the end, General Crook recommended him for West Point, and he went. He didn't have much choice. What else could he have done? After he graduated, he worked his way up to the rank of major in the Army, and then he met Leigh Enderson.

He married her and left the Army. He worked for J.P. Morgan, and then he had a hand in her death. Stryker released a long-labored breath that ended with "Fuck." He took a big gulp of the hot coffee, burning his mouth on purpose. Should have checked the gun settings. It was his fault. He would never forget and never live it down. Leigh lived in his brain with good and bad memories. The bad ones haunted him: her bloodied, gun-powdered, blackened body. She had said his name as he held her. It was her last word before she died, and it rode on blood that bubbled from her mouth. He couldn't let her memory die, not ever.

For three months after Leigh's death, Stryker drank, heavily. Then, he realized he could not, or more accurately, did not want to drown her memory in whiskey. He tried to remember only the good times, but the nightmares would not let him. Eventually, he decided he had to live with them. He deserved the damn things. At least they kept her memory alive. She lived in the dreams, and he did not want to kill them.

Stryker finished the coffee before he realized the cable cars had shut down for the night. He returned the empty cup to a deserted counter and went outside to hail a horse cab. After waiting another half-hour, knew the cabs had stopped running, too. He started up Market Street toward the Palace Hotel, a mile on foot. Naturally, the chilly rain fell harder. He turned up his collar under the Stetson. It was as if someone above hated people in the city and was trying to wash them into the bay. "Why else would it rain so damn much in San Francisco?" Stryker groused aloud. If it were not for Hearst and Morgan—well, Morgan—he would not have come to the city.

Then, after almost falling twice, it dawned on him, that slick-soled western boots were not proper footwear for walking on wet, cobblestone streets. Carlito's, a bar was still open; it was about halfway to the hotel on a corner lot of Market and Beale. Soft guitar music flowed out the open door. *Why the hell not?* He entered and sat at a table for two a few feet from the open door. The room was empty except for him, a guitar player, and a waitress and bartender, who talked with one another behind the liquor counter in the back. The room was not well-lit. Two kerosene lanterns on each side wall provided light. It was a small room, no more than twelve feet wide and twenty feet deep. Two-person tables lined the side walls. There was a door halfway down the left wall, flat against the wall and closed. Stryker surmised the side door led outside. It could be a staircase out there. The bar was two-story. A half-circular stage that was only twelve inches high was in a back corner where the male guitarist sat on a chair strumming a soft Spanish melody. A chest-high bamboo bar with a black leather crown occupied the opposite corner where the waitress and bartender congregated. Shelving behind the bar held wine and liquor bottles. There was no chilled beer and no chilled wine. A pot of hot water rested on a metal frame with a lit candle beneath it. The bartender was a solidly built forty-looking fellow, who was clean-shaven and mostly bald. He stood behind the bar, wiping down the counter. A painting hung on the rear wall depicting a forest of ship masts in the San Francisco Bay. Ship owners abandoned their vessels in the harbor and were sunk in place. Over forty ships would eventually lie beneath the city's financial district after the landfill extended the waterfront into the bay.

It took a long time for the waitress to come out from behind the bar. Even in the dim light, it was apparent she was annoyed. Stryker figured she and the bartender were deciding whether they would still serve drinks or close for the night. She sauntered to Stryker's table. She appeared to be in her early thirties, a little overweight, and wore no make-up, of course. Women, except for prostitutes, had not begun to wear it in the 1880s. This one's face looked tired and washed out. She could have used a little color. It would have helped.

"Something hot," Stryker growled, chilled from the rain.

"Hot-buttered rum." The waitress spun around and sauntered back to the bar.

Stryker did not argue. He'd not had the drink before, but she said it was hot. It seemed appropriate for a cold, rainy night. He heard what sounded like a metal spoon stirring in a glass behind the bar.

Carrying the drink in a glass mug, on a round wooden tray, the waitress brought the steaming rum drink to Stryker's table. "Seventy-five cents. Pay the bartender before you leave. No seconds." *Miss Cheerful* returned to the bar, grabbed a purse from behind, and walked past Stryker, to the door. "Good night, Earl." She closed the door behind her.

Earl stayed busy cleaning up around the bar. It suited Stryker, he wanted to be alone. The rum drink was hot. Too hot to go down fast. Good and hot, but too sweet for his taste. A little too girly. The rain pounded the outside walls when the wind blew against the wood. No sense in rushing the rum. Stryker settled back in the chair, leaving his arm stretched on the table and his fingers loosely gripping the mug's handle.

The door opened behind him. Stryker glanced and spotted a woman, about five-nine. She was slim, but it was hard to tell for sure under her raincoat. The slanted rain cap covered much of her face. He watched her stroll to the bar, and he heard her say in an accent, "Give me what he's drinking."

Earl complied without a grumble.

They must know one another, Stryker thought. *What is she doing out this time of night?* He sat straighter in the chair and slid the drink closer to him. He lifted the glass and sipped the rum, watching the woman as she waited for her drink. Earl struck a match under the pot that he had extinguished earlier while cleaning up. Would have thought ole' Earl might have complained a bit. She removed the rain hat and laid it on the bar. She kept her back to Stryker.

It took about three minutes. The water had to re-heat and neither Earl nor the woman spoke while the drink was made. Earl finally took the pot from the flame and poured hot water into a mug which he had partly filled with the rum and butter. Earl stirred the mixture and then pushed the mug across the counter to the woman. She lifted it to her nose, sniffed the concoction, and took a sip. Apparently satisfied, she turned and started across the floor toward Stryker's table.

She wore make-up. Even in the dimly lit room, Stryker saw it. Not too much; it was tastefully applied. Without the rain cap, she was more like five-seven. Her black hair hung straight. When she reached Stryker's table, she placed her glass on the table and took off the raincoat. She slung it on an adjacent chair and sat across from him. She was thin, had angular facial features, and was dark-skinned, with eyes black as coal. She could have been anywhere between twenty-five to thirty-five years old. She had been around. Lines on her face suggested a story. Flickering lantern light danced across her face, exaggerating the sharpness of her cheekbones. In short, the woman had an aura of mystery and a no-nonsense air about her. The type of face seen in dime novels depicting an evil, villainous woman. Another man might have been intimidated. Stryker was intrigued. She lifted her glass and took a sip of the hot drink, all the while staring at Stryker. *If she is a prostitute, she has a unique way of selling it,* Stryker mused to himself.

Neither spoke and both remained staring at each other until their glasses were almost empty. Then she said, "Would you like another?"

"No." Stryker could have finished the last of the rum and left. He could have, but he was intrigued.

"Curious why I sat with you?"

"Prostitute."

"No."

He was relieved she wasn't a hooker, although most were not particularly bad, personality-wise, that is. "What do you want?"

"Want? Nothing. Want me to leave?"

"No."

"Take off your hat. I can't see your face," she ordered.

Normally, Stryker would not take orders like that from anyone. But it was deep into a cold and rainy night. *Ah hell…* Stryker took off the Stetson.

"You look mean."

"Look in the mirror, lady." Stryker meant to just think that. He'd not realized he said it until it was too late. *Fuck.* He *was* tired and ornery.

Her smile would have broken the glass in the mirror. The abrupt change was startling. Warm and friendly. It caught Stryker off-guard, and he was unable to mine a proper response.

"I use one to put on make-up." The smile lingered.

Her accent was French maybe. "Reckon I shouldn't have said that," Stryker admitted. He wasn't being contrite. Not Stryker. He was just stating a fact. "Why you out late in the rain?"

"My work. What's your name?"

"Stryker, and yours's."

"Rawlings"

That must be her last name, Stryker thought. "You work, Rawlings?"

"Yes." The smile faded.

"What kind?" Stryker asked it as a question. Uncharacteristic of him.

"Can't tell you."

"Top secret." He was being sarcastic.

"Yes, it is."

"Don't tell me, then."

"I won't. But if I were to slip and tell you, I would need to guarantee your silence, maybe fuck you to death." The smile returned, though it was a bit strained. "Right now, I'm tired, chilled to the bone, and not drunk enough." She clutched her glass and swigged a big gulp of rum.

Tough girl. Stryker thought momentarily of pressing her to tell. The woman *was* kind of alluring. "Yes, I would like another rum."

"Me too."

They talked about less important things. She was from Belgium and had been in the United States for five years. She revealed that she had been born stateside, though. Her English was good, but she had a noticeable accent. Her work had something to do with government. Stryker hinted his work was also with the government. Neither revealed more about their jobs. That was two things they had in common. They did secretive work and weren't members of the beautiful people crowd. They found out each had deceased spouses. Neither asked about the deaths. Two more things in common. Eventually, they finished their second drink, and the rain let up. Stryker rose first. He left four dollars on the table to cover the four drinks, put on the Stetson and offered a simple finger salute on the brim. He received a short nod in return, and he walked out of Carlito's, wondering who she was. The mystery deepened. He didn't even get her first name. He also admitted he wouldn't mind running into her again —just to satisfy his curiosity, of course.

A little farther up Market Street, Stryker remembered he'd read that virtuous European women wore make-up, in addition to those ladies who might have been a tad deficient in virtue. Four blocks away from the Palace Hotel, Stryker realized it must have been approaching three o'clock in the morning. Time in Carlito's was not well spent. He should have continued to the hotel without stopping at the bar and gotten more sleep. At least the rain had stopped. *What's Hearst got for me this time?* Stryker wondered.

Stryker walked past waiting horse cabs lined up on Market Street and entered the Palace's elegant grand court. The carriage entrance was an indoor roundabout for the rich and famous who visited the hotel. The entrance allowed guests to step from carriages and proceed directly to the magnificent hotel lobby without being subjected to the city's notoriously foul weather.

The Palace Hotel was known as the finest hotel in the world when it opened in 1875. William Ralston built the hotel, financed by his shaky banking empire. Before it opened, Ralston's Bank of California failed, and he went bankrupt. He drowned in the bay the same day he lost control of the Palace. Many people speculated he committed suicide. The hotel opened two months after his death. The Palace was one of the first hotels in the world to have elevators for the seven-story building. They called them *rising rooms* then. The redwood-paneled hydraulic elevators carried guests to each of the seven floors. It is unsure if Ralston ever got to ride one. As they say, sometimes you get the elevator, sometimes you get the shaft. Ol' Will got the shaft. His widow, Elizabeth, was bought out with $50,000 for the entire property.

Eight stories of white columned balconies overlooked the grand court. Each guest room had an electronic call button to satisfy every whim, and each had private bathrooms with bathtubs and flushable toilets. All the guestrooms were thoughtfully designed to be joined if needed. The parlors had large bay windows, providing excellent views of the city.

Stryker strode across the marble floor of the expansive, high-ceiling lobby with a gleaming crystal chandelier, to the front desk. An imposing twenty-six-foot wide, six-foot high mahogany counter had twelve waist-high windows for customers and desk clerks. The Palace Hotel referred to guest relations staff as attachés.

"Good morning, Mister Stryker," the attaché greeted. The regular hotel staff, those who had been around for a while, knew the mixed breed and that he was to be accorded special treatment upon orders from Senator George Hearst. Hearst, who often resided at the hotel in a reserved suite on the eighth floor, was given special privileges, being that he was a close friend of Senator William Sharon, who owned the Palace.

Stryker nodded in return. He was tired, wet, and chilled; his clothes were still damp from the rain. "Got a room?"

"Yes, sir," the attaché cheerfully replied. He wore a bright red waistcoat, white shirt, red bowtie, and tan slacks with red pipping down the sides. "Here is your key," he said, holding out a shiny brass key.

"I'll meet Hearst for breakfast. Tell me when and where." Stryker said, taking the key.

The desk clerk looked down at a notepad on the counter and ran his finger down the scribblings. "In the men's grill, sir, eight o'clock."

Stryker turned and headed to the *rising rooms*. Not many guests wandered about this time of night, only those well-lubricated and not cognizant of the late hour. Walking past the men's grill, he spied four men still drinking and smoking cigars. No women, just men drinking and smoking. A young man and woman wobbled their way to the elevator, arm in arm. Stryker suspected they had imbibed extensively as well, enjoying their young lives, rigors of responsibility not yet burdensome. He figured they were in their early twenties; they could have been a year or two either way. The boy was clean-shaven with wavy black hair and lively eyes. The girl was a strawberry blonde, also with lively eyes. Hers were green. Stryker joined them on the elevator.

"What floor, please?" the operator asked the couple, who were still hanging on to each other and sporting impish grins. The uniformed attendant had worked at the hotel long enough to know Stryker always went to the eighth floor. He didn't ask him.

"Fifth floor, sir," the boy replied, giving the girl a playful smile. She glanced at Stryker who was watching her, and she erased the smile and lowered her eyes to the floor. Stryker supposed their evening was not over. They were young. He was never that young. Leigh was. Leigh enjoyed life. *Yeah, until I killed her.* Sudden memories of his long-dead wife sobered his face and made it look longer, older, and angrier. When the girl saw Stryker staring at her, she must have thought he was being critical. He was, but not of her. The rising room stopped on the fifth floor. The operator drew back the expanding brass gate. The young couple excited arm in arm and hurried down the hallway. The gate closed.

"Eighth floor, sir." Stryker stepped out onto the thick, green carpeting and checked the number on the brass key. *812.* He walked to the room, inserted the key in the door, and opened it. It was not his normal room; nevertheless, it was like his regular one. It had dark green carpeting, dark wood furniture, a king-size bed, and a black and white tiled bathroom. He dropped the saddlebag on the floor and went to the bathroom. He turned on the hot water in the clawfoot bathtub and added soap. It felt good to finally get the sticky, wet clothes off. By the time he stripped, the tub was half full. He grabbed a towel off the rack and laid it on a chair near the bathtub.

David Buick developed the process of binding porcelain to cast iron in the early 1880s, and it was that tub model Stryker got into. He settled into the hot soapy water, relaxed a bit, and then began soaping himself. He would have taken more time, but that bed in the next room looked pretty good. He recalled when an old-timer stood next to Stryker, watching a burial. He had remarked, "That hole is looking *pretty good." Poor bastard must have been worn out.*

Stryker finished his bath, got out of the tub, dried off, and grabbed the white terrycloth robe off a brass hook. It was too short. It only came down to mid-thigh. *Fuck it, going to bed.*

He draped the robe over the footrail, pulled back the maroon bedcover, and slipped between the cool satin sheets. It felt damn good. *Four hours of this.* Those were Stryker's last thoughts before he fell asleep.

The mixed breed did not sleep well, though. Nightmares wouldn't leave him alone, even when extremely tired. He is not capable of getting deep sleep. In the Army, he learned to sleep lightly, as if a part of his brain remained awake, ready to alert him to danger. But in the thin layer of slumber's twilight, nightmares dwell.

CHAPTER FOUR

nother one.

The bedroom scene appeared out of nowhere, the way dreams do. They just happen with no introduction.

The scene took place in a hotel room. Stryker awakened. It was the dead of the night. Leigh, his wife, stood in the middle of the floor, wearing a thin white nightgown and staring at the door. Her body was silhouetted by the moonlight coming through a window. Strands of her golden hair glistened. The moon was not normally so bright that it lit up hair, but it could in a dream. Stryker rose from the bed, and he lit a candle that was on the nightstand. He carried the candle to Leigh. She was frightened. He held the candle higher. She was trembling, and her horrified expression was strangely highlighted by the candlelight.

"What's wrong, Leigh?"

"I'm scared."

"Of what?"

"Outside the door."

"Did you hear something?" Stryker asked.

They communicated without moving their lips, the way people do in dreams.

"No."

Stryker pulled his Colt.45 from the nightstand and approached the door. He opened it and looked outside. The hallway was empty. He returned to Leigh, and while holding the gun, he wrapped his arm around her shoulders. "Come back to bed, sweetheart. There's no one out there."

"No, I can feel it."

"Feel what, Leigh?"

"Something bad."

"Something bad?"

"Something bad is going to happen."

"No, sweetheart. Nothing bad is going to happen. I won't let it."

Leigh stared at Stryker and offered a fractured smile without saying anything.

"Come on. Let's go back to bed."

"I'm scared."

"Leigh, there's nothing to fear. No one was outside the door. If there was, I'd put a big hole in 'em with this gun." Stryker waved the.45 so Leigh could see it. "I've got a big day tomorrow, you know, the firepower demonstration. If it goes well, it will mean a huge contract for the company, make it, and us a lot of money."

"I'm sorry, Stryker. I didn't mean to wake you," Leigh said. But she was still shaking.

"That's okay. Now, c'mon. Let's get some sleep." Stryker nudged Leigh on the shoulder and guided her back to bed. He put the gun away, and they got under the covers. Stryker put an arm under and around Leigh's neck and caressed her forehead. "Now, go to sleep, Leigh. I'm here. It'll be all right. I won't let anything happen."

He gently circled his fingers on Leigh's temple, hoping to relax her. Later, he heard her sniffling and knew she was crying. Sleep would not come for a long time for either of them.

The firepower demonstration took place the following day. Stryker oversaw the event. It did not go well. A man named Bauer, an unscrupulous business competitor, changed the firing coordinates that had been given to the Howitzer battery's firing team. An adjusting round landed out of the safety zone. It killed Leigh and all her family who were having a picnic in what was supposed to be a safe area. Stryker found Leigh dying from the shrapnel wounds. Her body was blackened with gunpowder and bleeding badly. He rushed to her and lifted her torso. Leigh opened her eyes, looked at him, and said his name on a rivulet of blood flowing from her mouth.

Stryker killed Bauer–the reason Stryker was wanted for murder. He blamed himself for Leigh's death because he failed to ensure the firing coordinates were correct. He was so eager to show the artillery's new indirect firing ability that he neglected to double-check the coordinates. His failure cost his wife her life. He had never lost, nor would he ever lose the crushing guilt.

Stryker woke drenched in sweat. It was seven in the morning. He rolled over, and no one else was there. For the briefest of moments, he half thought he might see Leigh beside him. It took a second for him to realize where he was. *You're in the Palace Hotel in San Francisco. Leigh's dead.* Stryker sat up and tried to think, tried to remember. Yes, he and Leigh had stayed in a hotel the night before the firepower demonstration. It was a long time ago. *The dream? Real? Shit. Don't know.* Stryker rubbed his face, frustrated he couldn't remember that night or what happened. For sure, the next day was real.

He swung his feet to the floor and grunted a groan as he got out of bed. Breakfast was at eight with Hearst. He stumbled to the bathroom, still thinking about the dream and groggy from getting less than four hours of sleep. It was not yet daylight outside, so he flipped a light switch[1]. Stryker placed his hands on the sink and leaned close to the mirror. He studied the weathered face in the glass. "You're the man who killed her." He dropped his head and blew out a long breath. He

---

1. The California Electric Light Company brought electricity to the city's street lamps and the Palace Hotel in 1879. A Jesuit Priest founded the company.

took another deep breath and lifted his face to the mirror. "Well, get on with it. You've got a meeting to go to."

Stryker washed his face, cleaned his teeth, shaved around the short beard, wet his hair, and ran fingers through it. It was his routine. He put memories on hold while completing his toiletries.

Stryker didn't allow self-recriminations to interfere with duty, work, or responsibilities, at least not during the day, and not at night when working a job. However, after one of those damn nightmares, that's when it hit him. They always reminded him of his failure. He wore the guilt like a heavy overcoat he couldn't take off. He tried to tell himself that at least he saw her in dreams, but it was no good. No good at all. After all the years, he would never get over Leigh's death, nor would he ever shed his guilt. Until he died, he would always live with grief and guilt.

There were many graves in Stryker's graveyard. Most of them lie unmarked on the ground. A few lay under marble headstones with the names of the dead etched on them. One special grave was in a large, beautifully well-tended mausoleum. The name above the entrance read, *Leigh Enderson.*

Guests were already lined up at the massive front desk, waiting to check out when Stryker walked across the lobby floor to the men's grill room. He wore the Peacemaker in his gun belt. He had no plans to use it. But it did serve to diminish small talk. He need not have worried over unwelcome conversations. His fierce countenance kept most would-be conversationalists at bay.

Travelers from all over the world came to the grill room to dine and do business. The best steaks and chops were on the menu along with the finest libations from the elegant marble top, cherry-wood bar. White linen covered the tables, and chairs were abundantly padded for male derrieres in expensive suits. Electric ceiling lights provided ample lighting to read lavish menus for the most sophisticated palates.

The men's grill room was forty by sixty feet, had a twenty-foot ceiling, and large wall mirrors, making the room seem even larger. The walls were covered in ornately carved mahogany paneling. There was a liquor bar along the left wall. A heavy layer of cigar smoke blanketed the room. It was a man's eatery. Booths along the side walls had curtains just in case a fellow had a lady friend and did not want to be seen wantonly breaking the rules or if he required discretion and did not wish to be recognized with a woman who was not his wife. Other men in the grill room extended the courtesy of acceptance for they might need such consideration in the future.

The grill room captain informed Stryker that Senator Hearst had yet to arrive. However, he sat Stryker in the senator's usual curtained booth along the side wall. Five minutes after he sat down, Hearst joined him.

George Hearst was a slim six feet in height, ramrod straight, and in his midsixties. Stryker had watched him come to the table and gave the senator a nod when he sat down. Hearst saved him from being chopped to death by angry loggers and then paid Stryker handsomely for securing the *San Francisco Examiner.* The dollar amount paid was one hundred thousand dollars. Hearst gave the newspaper to William Randolph Hearst, his son. Hearst had his own brush with the law. He had killed a man in Park City, apparently with good cause, since he was not charged. He and Stryker got along well.

George Hearst was nothing like the scoundrel portrayed more than a century later. A principled man with unquestioned integrity, he is well-liked by the five thousand men who worked for him. The men called him "George." Hearst made his fortune honestly buying and selling mining properties, with no hint of extortion, or soiled with dishonor. He was a lifelong friend of Leland Stanford. Far from being miserly with money, he gave generously to strangers in need and was the primary source of funding for the early construction of the University of California, Berkley. The modern entertainment industry has portrayed George and his son, William, as bad men; it is a gross disservice to them. One must wonder why their reputations were so savagely besmirched. The Hearst men were not like that at all.

"Morning, Stryker." The senator was familiar with the mixed breed's taciturn nature. He did not expect a warm greeting in return. Both men ordered coffee from the waiter who had followed Hearst to the table. Neither man broke the silence until the coffee arrived and the first sips were taken. The men were not given to small talk.

"What do you think about ghosts?" Hearst asked.

"Haven't seen any." Stryker chose not to mention those he saw in dreams.

"An entire family, the Bosworths, was slaughtered last week, husband, wife, and two children, ages seven and ten." Hearst, who had been fingering the cup, brought it to his mouth and took another sip of the hot brew before continuing. "Neighbors saw two men walk out the front door before the victims were discovered. Police arrested the two men and charged them with murder."

Stryker listened while drinking his coffee.

"I don't think they did it," Hearst said.

Stryker placed his cup back on its saucer.

"The Bosworth bodies were discovered later in the morning by three maids who went into the house to clean." Hearst sipped coffee again, then continued. "The maids found the bodies in the kitchen after being in the house for over an hour. They said they'd heard talking and stuff being moving around upstairs but didn't see anyone on the upper floors. It wasn't until they came downstairs to the kitchen that they saw the bodies. Husband and wife tied up. Throats cut, kids too. The women fled the house, yelling and screaming. They ran into a policeman down the street." Hearst set down his cup. "Here's where it gets more interesting. The policeman didn't want to enter the house alone, so he rounded up two more officers to go in with him. It took another twenty minutes, he said. Then, they went in the front door, which was left open by the maids. When they got to the kitchen, the bodies were gone. No bodies, no blood, but none of the Bosworths have been seen since, dead or alive. Neighbors, including my wife, Phoebe, say they can hear voices coming from the house late at night. Oh, it's been searched... many times and by different investigators who have found nothing."

"They *are* dead," Stryker asked in his customary statement.

"Could be a macabre hoax, but I don't think so. All three maids were scared shitless. It's true, the police found no blood in the house, however, they are sure the family's been murdered, and the bodies have been taken somewhere."

"Taken somewhere," Stryker repeated.

"Hmmm, the police think the two men they arrested had accomplices. More than two killers in the house, and somehow, they cleaned up the blood and got rid of the bodies. Maybe they figure no bodies, no crime, I guess," Hearst said. "How they did it without being seen is a mystery. There were two hours between the two men who were seen running out of the house and the maids arriving. So, they did have time to clean up the kitchen and move the bodies."

"What's this have to do with me?" Stryker politely asked a question.

"Lambert Bosworth and his wife Beatrice were close friends of mine." Hearst drew a deep breath before continuing. "They rented the house next to me on Nob Hill. They were wealthy; Hank made his money in the stock market. Damned awful what happened to them." Hearst gritted his teeth and shook his head. "Stryker, they have a niece named Kate, Kate Bosworth, who is now beneficiary to the trust. According to their lawyer, She's on her way out of Boston. She'll be here in three days."

"Would you gentlemen like to order breakfast?" asked the waiter who had approached the table. "It's starting to get busy, and we thought you might want to order your breakfast, so you won't have a long wait." The waiter, young and freshly scrubbed, looked a bit nervous. The head waiter had told him to interrupt Stryker and the senator to take their orders.

Hearst gave the lad a scornful glance, then turned to Stryker. "Go ahead, Stryker."

"Steak and eggs, toast. More coffee."

"I'll have my usual," Hearst told the waiter, leaving the young man to find out what "usual" meant.

"Thank you." The waiter left to locate the grill captain.

"Now, where the hell was I?" Hearst asked, eyeing the waiter as he walked away.

Before the senator could recollect his thoughts, Stryker helped him out, "What you want from me."

"Oh yeah, I want you to find out what's happened to the Bosworth home before Kate gets here. And find out who killed them; I want to make sure they're punished."

"The two men in jail. What were they doing in the house?" Stryker asked, politely again.

"They said they planned a burglary but left when they saw the murders."

"Could be the two were part of a burglary gang and got cold feet after the killings, and the other gang members moved the bodies."

"That's what the police think," Hearst said, nodding.

"But you don't."

"I have doubts."

"The voices in the mansion."

"Yes. The police have been to the house twice and have heard nothing. They've charged the two men with murder, and plan to ask for the death penalty, prison time if the men talk."

"And you want me to spend time at the house." Stryker leaned back from the table.

"I can arrange for you to interview the men in jail if you like, then yes. I want you to go to the mansion, do a search, and even spend a few nights in the place. See what you can find."

"The police are not going to help."

"No, they think they have the killers, two of them anyway. They've been to the house, looked in every corner, so they say. They said there's nothing else to find there, and they're gonna be busy with the railroad strike in three days."

"Railroad strike."

"That's right. Expecting quite a fight. Both sides gearing up for one. Stryker, Morgan's in Lead, South Dakota. Should be back about then."

"Unless there's a strike."

"Unless there's a strike," Hearst repeated. "That's right."

"Get me in to talk with the two men. I want the address and keys to the house. One more thing, where can I get information about the Bosworth family, friends, associates, enemies."

"Hmmm, Lambert Bosworth, and his wife, Beatrice were prominent members of society here in San Francisco. I imagine you could search the society pages of newspapers in the library for public information. For private dealings, Lambert's office is on California Street, next to the San Francisco Stock and Bond Exchange. I don't know the exact address, Stryker, but his company is *Bosworth Securities*." Hearst finished the last of his coffee, and set the empty cup on the saucer, indicating he wanted the cup refilled. "You should find that name on a door or building there. His office manager or secretary may still be in the office. Someone to speak with, I think. Don't know a name." He idly spun the cup on the saucer and pensively cocked his head as he added. "I'm not sure how the police questioned them. That is about all I know, Stryker. Who knows, Lambert may have had enemies. He was a stockbroker. Not all stocks made money." Hearst gave the cup a rest.

Stryker took note of Hearst's pondering. If the police thought they had the killers in jail, they may not have inquired further. Burglary is a simple motive. *But why kill the entire family?* He suspected there was more to the story.

"I'll make the arrangements. Is tomorrow soon enough, Stryker?" Hearst got a nod for a reply, and then he spied a waiter headed to their table and carrying a tray. "Ah here comes breakfast."

The server, whose name tag read, "Franklin," set the silver tray on the table. He put a plate with biscuits and sausage covered with gravy in front of Hearst and gave Stryker a plate of eggs, sunny side up, and a slab of steak. Stryker had this breakfast often and uttered a small grunt of satisfaction. The yolks were basted with a healthy smattering of hot fat, eggs cooked how he liked them.

"Would you gentlemen like any juice or more coffee?" Franklin asked, slipping the tray under his arm.

"Coffee for both," Hearst said. After the waiter left, he broke open a biscuit with his fork, and told Stryker, "I'll have a police officer pick you up later this afternoon, say around three o'clock. Meet him in the lobby. When you return from jail, I want you to visit the house by tomorrow at the latest."

The rest of the conversation was Hearst grousing about government bureaucracies he had to deal with. He didn't ask Stryker about speaking to the jailed men or what he would do in the mansion. The senator had learned not to ask for details. He often heard secondhand reports that Stryker was always around violence, killings, and questionable doings. Nevertheless, he let Stryker handle matters his way. His methods *were* successful, and Hearst did not want to know the particulars.

Stryker finished eating his breakfast quicker than Hearst. Stryker never thought eating was a social event. When finished, he rose from the table and walked from the grill with only the tip of the Stetson as a salutation. Hearst was not offended. He knew the man.

In the carriage turnabout, Stryker hailed a horse cab. "Take me to Pacific Hall on Bush Street," he told the driver. He had been to the nascent public library before and knew it kept prior newspaper publications. He decided to visit the library since *The Examiner* wasn't the only published newspaper in San Francisco. There was also the *Elevator, Daily Report, Pacific Rural Press, Star,* and a couple other lesser-read newspapers. They came and went. The *Examiner* survived.

When Stryker was dropped off at Pacific Hall, he learned the library had been relocated to a wing of city hall on Larkin Street, near Grove and Hyde Streets. *Shit.* He hailed another cab. "Take me to Pacific Coast Stock Exchange on Pine Street." He'd visit the library later.

It took a while, but Stryker located Bosworth Securities on the second floor of a five-story brick building next to the stock exchange. That is where the address plaque by the main entrance said it was anyway. No rising room in this building. He climbed two flights to the second floor and walked down the hall, passing etched names on glass doors until he came to one that read Bosworth Securities. It was unlocked, and he entered.

"Mister Jonas!" A young girl with freckles and red hair in a ponytail sat at the front desk. She called for her boss when Stryker came through the door. The reception room was approximately twenty feet square, and walnut paneled with a large picture of the New York Stock Exchange hanging on the wall opposite the receptionist's desk. Her call to Jonas was more urgent than her usual ones for assistance. Samual Jonas took over as securities licensed principal and office manager the day after Lambert Bosworth was murdered. An open doorway behind the receptionist's desk led to a thirty-foot walnut-paneled hallway with office doors on each side of the hall. Portraits of company officers hung on the walls. The doors, top half glass, bottom half solid mahogany, had engraved men's names in the glass. At the far end of the hall, there was an open bay of plain wooden desks. Stryker couldn't see how many. Men sat at the desks he could see, and a new form of communication, the telephone, was on top of every desk. The first door in the hallway slung open, hard, rattling the glass, and Samuel Jonas rushed out.

Jonas noticed Stryker standing in the reception room and he stopped in the hallway. Stryker did not look like a typical stock investor. The tall man appeared none-too-friendly, and wore a gun, a Colt.44. Jonas stayed in the hallway to address him. One could assume Jonas wanted to be able to scurry back into his office if things did not go well.

"What can we do for you, sir?" Jonas asked with a little quiver in his voice.

The salutation briefly reminded Stryker of his officer days in the Army. Being addressed as *sir* did not come with the same respect these days. Jonas added trepidation and that carried some respect.

"Got a few questions about Bosworth."

"Well, mister, I don't know if…"

"Who might you be, sir?" the receptionist quickly asked, heading off a risky response from Jonas. He was having a little trouble with the right words. She correctly suspected Stryker could be touchy and Jonas might antagonize the.44. Often, a woman can be more courageous than a man, especially if she senses a man won't be as eager to get nasty with a woman, a young and pretty woman. She did not know the mixed breed, but no matter this time.

"Name's Stryker. Official inquiry."

"Official?" Jonas recovered a bit.

"Who knew Bosworth best? That you?" Stryker stepped past the reception desk, took Jonas by the arm, and led him down the hall.

By this time more hallway doors were open. Men's heads poked out. "It's all right, gentlemen," Jonas said. "This officer just wants to ask me a few questions about the murders. Go about your work." Jonas opened his office door. "Please step inside, Stryker, where we can talk." Once in Samuel's office, Jonas went behind a six-foot wide, highly polished, and stained black oak desk. Jonas swiveled the black leather, wingback chair around and sat. He angled a glance down at a side drawer and quickly returned his attention to Stryker. "Please, have a seat, Mister Stryker, and call me Samuel."

Stryker sat in one of the two brown leather chairs facing the desk. They were smaller than Samuel's. The stockbroker appeared in his early forties and nurtured a baby paunch. Samual was prematurely bald, and his facial rosacea suggested he spent time in the bar after the stock market closed. Samuel was a sharp dresser in his navy-blue, pin-striped suit, sterling cuff links, and pink flowered tie with a tie bar. A cigar box, silver cutter, and ashtray sat next to a leather writing pad. A quill pen, ink bottle, and an ornate glass lamp were also on the desk.

"You made two good decisions," Stryker said flatly.

"Excuse me. What do you mean?"

"The first was getting me in this office to talk privately. The second was not pulling out that gun."

Samuel's face reddened. "Yes, I guess I did." Jonas cracked a weak smile, clasping his hands together on the desk pad. "Well, Mister Stryker, what questions can I answer for you?"

"Who hated Bosworth enough to kill him and his family?"

"That is a rather difficult topic of discussion." Jonas leaned back in his chair. He clasped his hands on his chest like a person does when making a thoughtful decision.

"I can encourage the discussion."

"I don't want my family killed, too, Mister Stryker." Jonas squirmed uncomfortably in the chair. "I don't know who you are."

Stryker grasped the implication. "I would only kill you."

"If you're not with them, who are you? You don't look like the police."

"I have the cooperation of Commissioner O'Brien and Chief Brock," Stryker said. "And, Bosworth has neighbors who want answers. Another thing, Jonas, if I learn you're with them, I might reconsider killing your family."

"A private detective?"

"Close enough. I figure Bosworth got punished for something big." Stryker leaned closer. "You are aware of happenings there."

"Ghosts."

"Heard that."

"They haven't found the bodies, have they?" Jonas asked.

"Who punished Bosworth?"

"Don't know." Jonas sat up straighter. He was wrestling with it. "Look, I can only tell you where there's been, disagreements." He paused for a response. Didn't get it. "We were to bring an IPO for a new railroad company. An IPO is—"

"An initial public offering for a new company," Stryker supplied.

"Yes," Jonas said with a nascent smile. "And it caused, shall we say, disagreements. The new rail company was to be non-union. The railroad companies we have now are all union." Jonas leaned forward, resting his clasped hands together on the desk. "Are you familiar with union shops, Mister Stryker?"

"Know about 'em."

"Another thing, Taggert Railways, the new company was to lay standard gauge rails with a new kind of steel, replacing the narrow-gauge rails, trains run on today. Narrow gauge is—"

"Three feet, six inches, and four-feet, eight and a half inches for standard. And the new steel is produced with non-union labor."

"You seem to know more about this more than I thought."

"Steel and rail, two powerful unions. Unions can sometimes be helpful for workers, but leadership is often corrupted and advocates Marxist ideology."

"Whoa! Now, you are familiar with…" Jonas broached a wide grin.

"Lambert was good friends, exceptionally good friends, with Henry Rearden, the owner of the new railroad company. Attempts on Rearden's life have been made too. Now that Lambert is dead, the IPO might not go forward. That would bankrupt Rearden, but maybe then they would leave him alone." Jonas blew out an exasperated breath. "I have probably said too much. But dammit, if those union men had something to do with the murders, they need to be caught and executed."

"Names."

"Even if I knew them, I wouldn't tell you. I've already told you too much. Besides, it might not be union men who did it." Jonas sat back in his chair. "And actually, I hope they weren't involved in the killings. I suppose, Mister Stryker, you will be considerate enough to not divulge any of what I have told you to anyone else."

Stryker nodded. "The noises coming from inside the house. Know anything about that?" Stryker extended the courtesy of asking the question as an interrogative.

"What kind of sounds?"

"Male and female voices."

"Like ghost sounds?"

"Yes."

"I only heard about it from Mrs. Hearst, a neighbor of the Bosworth's. Jonas rubbed his chin. "You know the Hearsts?"

"Familiar with her husband," Stryker replied. "Anything new, Jonas, I'll be at the Palace Hotel."

Samuel nodded twice. "Yes sir."

Stryker lifted from the chair and exited Samuel's office. He shut the door behind him and glanced down the hall. Men lined up in front of the open pit trading room. New investors itching to buy the latest new mining stock, which traded in "mine feet." Hearst had schooled Stryker on stock trading with mining shares. The senator made a fortune buying and selling mining stocks and had asked Stryker to invest with him on occasion. He did it three times. Lost on two, made a profit on one. After those three tries, Stryker rejected more proffered investments. It was too risky for him. But people said George Hearst had a nose for sniffing out productive gold and silver veins in rock. It was an uncanny gift. Stryker was more proficient in dealing with lead. He turned from the trading room and headed past the pretty receptionist to leave Bosworth Securities. He descended the stairs to street level. It was still mid-morning and Stryker did not need to return to the Palace until noon. The library would probably require more than two hours of research. Besides, Jonas had already given him a good lead.

CHAPTER FIVE

S tryker walked to the corner of California and Sansome Streets. There, he waited ten minutes to hop on the California Street cable car, and it was another ten-minute ride to Mason Street, where he stepped from the car.

The Mark Hopkins House was a spectacular six-story, 17,000-square-foot, Victorian mansion on fashionable Nob Hill where other multimillionaires of the Gilded Age built their homes. Hopkins was one of the Big Four (Hollis Huntington, Leland Standford, and Charles Crocker were the other three) who built the Central Pacific Railroad empire. The mansion's tower was the tallest point in the city. Mark built the mansion for his wife, Mary, who persuaded him to build it, but he died before it was completed in 1878. Then she remarried, moved to Massachusetts, built a 60,000-square-foot home, and left her $70 million estate to her second husband, Edward Searles, who was twenty-two years her junior. Could it be that Mary was a high-maintenance girl? Mark and Mary had no children of their own. They did adopt a son; however, Mary purposely excluded him in her will. If Mark had created a will or trust while he was alive, his estate might have been distributed more to his liking, alas, he left no such formal instructions. There is a lesson to be learned here.

After Edward Searles died, his nephew, Victor Searles, accused Edward, with ample evidence, of being a homosexual, which at the time, was a crime. Edward's suspected lover and constant companion, Arthur Walker, was left almost all of Edward's estate. *Ouch.*

The mansion was a multi-faceted, architectural marvel with tall towers, gables, peaked and domed roofs, and cloud-tickling spires. A wooden, monstrous beast on the hill, it did not survive the post-earthquake fire of 1906. However, in the late 1880s, it stood as an outstanding example of achievement and wealth. Incidentally, the earthquake and fire destroyed all of the Big Four's Nob Hill mansions.

Stryker admired the mansion for a moment before strolling up to the front entrance. The door was locked. He started around the building to search for an unlocked entrance. Up close the structure was even more imposing and he glanced skyward every few steps to take it all in. He did find other doors, but they too were locked.

Strolling around the grounds, Stryker listened for unusual noises coming from inside. He heard none. Naturally, it began to rain. He approached a set of ten concrete steps that led down to the basement. The walls and steps were cinder blocks plastered with concrete. Moss grew on the concrete and made it extra slick, and after going down three steps, Stryker kept a hand on top of the wall until he reached the landing. Water poured down the steps and flooded the landing. Debris had plugged up the drain. Stryker's boots splashed in an inch of water as he made three long strides to the basement door. He tried the faded brass doorknob. It spun easily, too easily. Stryker booted the door with a hard kick, and it banged open with a clunk. The basement was dank with a heavy clammy smell. Lantern light from inside showed from behind a dark, large, and hulking silhouette of a man just inside the door.

"Dammit! What the fu—?" The man bellowed.

The burly man was six feet tall with a pockmarked face. He had a full beard and wore a black watch cap, denim shirt, and trousers. He dropped the large canvas sack he had slung over his shoulder. It sounded like dishes and dinnerware breaking when it hit the floor. The stout burglar backed away from the door, wringing an injured hand. "Who the hell are you?" A Raven knife[1] was stuck in his belt.

Another man behind him raised his lantern higher.

Stryker pulled the sai and powered forward, smashing the sai's pommel into the big man's forehead. He staggered back a step before crashing to the floor.

The second male holding the lantern didn't see what happened to his partner. He stared at the big man on the floor. "Hey, what-cha do to Rafer?"

Flipping the sai in a blur, Stryker leaped over Rafer and rammed the center tine in the second man's mouth.

The burglar fell back against a wooden support post.

"Any more of you?" Stryker growled, keeping the sai jammed in between the man's teeth.

The burglar tried to shake his head. The sai pricking his throat stopped him. He lowered the lantern.

Stryker eased the sai from the man's mouth and pressed the tine against his tracheal notch. "Just you two?" Stryker pushed on the sai, drawing blood.

"Just us… two," the burglar rasped.

Stryker stuck the sai in the pouch behind his back and pulled the Peacemaker. He ordered the man to pull his dead partner's belt and tie his hands behind the post.

The thief bent over Rafer, unbuckled his belt, and slipped it off. He fisted the Raven knife and then released it upon hearing the Peacemaker's click. He rolled his partner over, shoved his hands under Rafer's armpits, and dragged him to the post. He pulled Rafer upright to tie him. "I think Rafer's dead."

"Back off," Stryker ordered, keeping the Colt pointed at the burglar. Stryker knelt and felt for a pulse. He shifted the gun to his left hand and pulled the razor from his pocket. He sank the blade under

---

1. Blade and handle made from a single piece of steel with a raven head forged on the handle

Rafer's left ear and ran it across his throat. Blood gushed from the gruesome gash. The big man coughed once.

Stryker wiped the blade on the dying man's shirt and stood. He ordered, "Upstairs."

The burglar turned and started toward the stairs by a far wall, holding the lantern in front of him. Stryker followed close behind.

They climbed up the stairs to a landing that had a closed door. Stryker prodded the burglar in the back with the Peacemaker, and the man opened the door.

The door opened under a staircase on the first floor.

"You want to go to the second floor?" The burglar asked, not turning around.

Stryker saw only a hallway and bedrooms rooms on the first floor. "Go."

The would-be thief guided Stryker to the second staircase leading to the next level. The light was better than in the basement, although not much better due to the heavy rain outdoors. The room they stepped into was huge with decorative walnut carvings on the walls, columns, and ceiling. There were at least half a dozen doorways leading to other rooms, two arched openings, others closed with ornate doors and brass hardware. An exceptionally large double door was at the end of a wide mahogany-paneled hallway. Three magnificent crystal chandeliers hung from the ceiling; the center light fixture was twice the size of the other two. Windows, framed by maroon-colored velvet curtains, stretched from the floor up to the twenty-foot ceiling. There was a massive stone fireplace with two emerald-green, tufted leather chairs in front of it. The wood rack built into the stone still held firewood. The rich know how to be lavish, Stryker mused. Another thing he noticed was that the furniture was sparse. No one had been living in the mansion after Mary moved back East until the Bosworths moved in, and they had not been there long. Mary may have taken the furniture with her, sold it off, or it was stolen. Regardless, the room was cold and sterile.

"Take me to the kitchen." Stryker motioned with the Peacemaker. "If we run into more robber friends, you'll get the first bullet."

The thief must have wondered what Stryker was up to, but he kept his mouth shut. They walked past the dining room, which had no table, and onto the kitchen. The swinging glass door hung open. The kitchen was also large, with two sinks, two stoves, and three center aisles for cutting, mixing, and serving preparations. Pots hung suspended on silver chains above each aisle table. There was no blood, just as the police reported.

Stryker stuck the gun barrel in the burglar's back. "This where you killed them?"

The robber attempted to turn around to Stryker. Thought better of it and asked, "Killed who?"

"The Bosworth family. You know who I mean," Stryker growled.

"No, we didn't kill anybody. This is the first time we been here. Honest. Rafer and me, we just got off the ship the day before yesterday. When were they—"

"What boat?" Stryker snarled.

"The *Wind Lass*! You can check. We were on it. Came from New York!" The man talked fast, thinking he might live.

Stryker shifted the Peacemaker to his left hand, pulled the razor, and slit the robber's throat. It would be safe to say, Stryker held thieves and murderers in the same regard. He watched the gagging man hit the floor but left the kitchen and returned to the parlor before the thief finished his dying.

The robber, would-be robber, was still choking on his blood when Stryker took a second look at the fireplace and decided to light a fire to dry his clothing. He found discarded newspapers, gathered kindling from the firewood rack, crumpled the paper under the grate, and crisscrossed pieces of kindling on the grating. Stryker carried matches, but not for smoking. He never smoked and thought those who purposefully drew smoke into their lungs were fools. The wood rack had boxed matches, and he used them, lighting the papers in three different sections on the edges. The paper lit, curling, burning black, smoking heavily until the chimney heated and began to draw the smoke. The kindling glowed on the edges, and he leaned down and blew on them until they started burning. Once the kindling caught fire, he added two split logs from the wood rack, crossing them as he did the kindling. Satisfied the fire had a good start, he settled into one of the leather chairs. About ten minutes later, he rose and put two more logs on the fire. It was a good fire, and he settled back in the chair.

The thief in the kitchen coughed once, loud enough to be heard over the crackling fire. Stryker didn't hear him after that. He propped his boots up on the hearth.

"What drives a man to achieve such wealth?" Stryker asked himself while staring at the fire. *Not the money. Money is just a byproduct,* he reasoned. It must be to achieve, to build, to make a mark in one's life. Inventors do not just dream of money. They dream of creating. Industrialists dream of industry empires. Doctors want to heal the sick. Banker's dream of creating wealth. That is different from making money to get rich. It is why factories are built, banks are started, the sick are healed, and light bulbs are invented. The big four in San Francisco built a railroad, the Central Pacific. Then, they got rich. A wife like Mary Hopkins thinks only of what money can buy, not what produces it. One can suppose she spent little time thinking about how the railroad made lives better. Others who dream of getting rich just to spend the money seldom become wealthy.

Stryker's ambition was wrung out of him early. Murderers with wanted posters throughout the land do not become captains of industry, brilliant inventors, doctors, or bankers. Although, some people might argue differently.

An ember escaped the fireplace and skittered onto the floor. Stryker used the fireplace shovel to scoop it up and pitch it back into the fire. He threw on another log and sank back into the chair.

CHAPTER SIX

November 22, 1864. The Georgia Militia had suffered heavy causalities while fighting General William T. Sherman's Army during his "March to the Sea." It was a brutal operation designed to destroy the South's infrastructure and eliminate not only its military's capacity to fight but also its will to fight. Sherman was, by most accounts, extraordinarily successful. The heavy fighting near the mid-Georgia town of Griswold Ville—about ninety-two miles southeast of Atlanta—had recently ended.

The southern landscape lay littered with dead, dying, and wounded, mostly southern men and boys. The North suffered thirteen killed and seventy-nine wounded. The Southern Milia had fifty-one men killed, 472 wounded, and 600 captured. It was not a good day for the South. The industrial town of Griswold Ville was destroyed and was never rebuilt after the war. Many of the wounded Southerners were not able to get medical treatment.

The right wing of Sherman's Army of Tennessee, commanded by Major General Oliver Howard had run into the Confederate Major General Joseph Wheeler's cavalry, drove them beyond Griswold Ville, and assumed a defensive position near Duncan's Farm.

A local farmhouse is where the eighteen-year-old Sergeant Neville

Stryker was drawn into the fighting. He served the entire time as one of six crew members on a Parrott Rifle, a twenty-pound field artillery gun, the largest used in the Civil War. Stryker began service as a private and earned promotions up to sergeant as other higher-ranking crew members were killed off. The Rebels targeted the gun crew to eliminate the weapon's devastating effectiveness on the battlefield. However, the Parrott Rifle was also notorious for unexpectedly blowing up and killing its crewmen.

The white, two-story farmhouse and barn was set on a little rise surrounded by one hundred and twenty-five acres of cotton fields. The cotton was not picked and was left to rot on the vines. The slave house, a single-story wooden building with one large room was vacant. It sat seventy-five yards down the hill, and away from the main house. The fifteen slaves who used to live in it left nine months before. They took off during the night and were never seen again by their owners, anyway. Only one male, Robert Dokes, the owner of the plantation remained on the property, and he was too old and sick to work the fields. Robert's wife had died three years earlier. His youngest daughter, Verity, thirty years of age, lost her husband two and half years prior during the Battle of Shiloh, Mississippi. She still lived in the main house to care for her father. Robert had a son, Bo, short for Beaufort, and another daughter other than Verity. That daughter's name was Amelia. Amelia, thirty-eight years old, was married with three children, ages nine, eleven, and nineteen. She lived in Savannah with her husband and children. Her husband was a lawyer and worked in his father's law office. Amelia visited the plantation by train to see her father and sister every six months, bringing her children with her. However, the trains had stopped due to the war. Elements of General Sherman's Army had blown up the tracks, heated the rails, and wrapped them around trees. They called them Sherman's neckties. Bo was in the Army, fighting for the South. Robert had not seen or heard from his son in two months.

It was past midnight when Sergeant Neville Stryker, with Corporal Jenson and two privates, Hunnicutt and Minshew, walked stealthily through a downpour, ten yards apart, carrying the muzzles of their

Spencer rifles down to keep the rain out of the barrels. Stryker led the men. They were headed toward the Dokes plantation on a reconnaissance mission to determine whether the house could be used as temporary headquarters for Major General Howard. Rebel snipers, belonging to a unit of Lieutenant General William J. Hardee, and having taken an awful beating by Howard's men, who carried Spencer repeater rifles, sought revenge. Despite outnumbering the Union forces, the Confederates carried Enfield rifle muskets and were no match for the Northern troops and their superior rifles.

Stryker and his men slogged through a muddy cotton field. Boots lifted from the mud with each step make sucking sounds in the rain. The men walked like drunkards, taking extra-long steps and trying to maintain their balance as they lifted their feet from the sticky red clay. At first, the grumbling behind Stryker was inaudible. The road to the Dokes house ran alongside the field and was firmer. The men cursed the mud, wanting to know why they weren't on the road. But the road, although more solid, ran on higher ground than the fields. Traveling on the road presented elevated profiles, which made them better targets for snipers. The downpour reduced visibility, making it more difficult for snipers to see targets, but that didn't matter to Sergeant Stryker. It was a risk he would not allow.

The cursing grew louder, the Corporal and Privates thought if they let their grumbling reach Stryker, he would change his mind about the road. Sergeant Stryker ignored them.

Private Minshew trudged in the mud ten feet behind the sergeant, Corporal Jenson, another ten feet behind him, and Hunnicutt brought up the rear, maintaining the ten-foot separation that Stryker ordered. It had been raining the past hour, and one could think it could not come down any harder, but it did. Corporal Jenson struggled to keep up with Stryker and Minshew. It rained harder and louder, and the corporal fell farther behind. Hunnicutt followed him.

Finally, Corporal Jenson growled, "Fuck it," and climbed up on the road. Private Hunnicutt saw Jenson's move, and thinking if his corporal got on the road, he could too, and he too scrambled to firmer footing.

A mile from the Dokes's house, the Georgia woods, tall, straight pine trees opposite open fields, stretched closer to the road. That is where the reconnaissance detail was now marching. Jenson and Hunnicutt marched quickly, almost catching up to Minshew and Stryker. Thirty yards behind Minshew, they were not close enough for Stryker to notice the two laggards on the road and getting an ass chewing. Minchew saw them and kept it to himself.

Two rifle shots rang out from the trees. One right after the other. The shots could have been thunder, but there was no lightning flash. Stryker threw himself to the road berm. He crawled up the berm to the road and readied the Spencer. Rain blurred his visibility, and he could only see trees across the road. He didn't see two bodies forty yards down the road. It was raining too hard. He looked left and saw Minshew crawling up to the road berm. Jenson and Hunnicutt weren't in sight.

Stryker backed off the berm, got on his feet, and slogged back to Minchew, crouching low and using the elevated road as cover. "See 'em?" Stryker asked after crawling up next to Minchew.

"No, nothing."

Stryker looked past Minchew. "I don't see Jenson and Hunnicutt."

"They're on the road."

"Shit."

Both bullets found their marks. Jenson took one, smashing through his ribs and his heart and killing him before he hit the road. Hunnicutt lay propped up on an elbow and was struggling to breathe. The bullet hit him in the throat, puncturing his windpipe. Blood rapidly filled his lungs.

"Stay here." Stryker slid off the edge and slogged another thirty yards back down the field. He crept up to the road and saw both men down. He heard Hunnicutt's coughing, and then the coughing stopped.

"You men all right?" Stryker called a muted yell, loud enough for the men to hear him but not carry to the trees. His anger at the two for not following orders did not override the concern for his men, even if the concern was about accomplishing the mission. He was still mighty pissed at the two men for disobeying him, though. He'd give them hell later, but they didn't answer him. *Shit!*

Stryker cradled the rifle in his elbows, crawled onto the road, and through the mud to Jenson. He was dead. Stryker wiggled off the road and sloshed ten more feet back to Hunnicutt. He found him dead, too. Twisting around in muddy rainwater, Stryker dropped back off the road.

"Stay off the fuckin' road 'til we get to the house," Stryker growled to Minshew.

"What 'bout Jenson and Hunnicutt?"

"They're dead."

Stryker and Minshew crouched low and slogged through the field until they got within two hundred yards of the Dokes's house. The rain let up to less than a downpour. The visibility improved. Stately oak trees lined both sides of the road. Then, the road spilled into a roundabout with a grass interior. Stryker and Minshew knelt behind a thick oak. They each took a side and peered around the tree.

"Use the trees," Stryker whispered. "If we take fire, go back." Stryker lost two men trying to find a comfortable bed for a general. Yes, it was their fault for getting on the road, but they wouldn't be lying dead in the mud if they had not been ordered by a staff officer currying favor for the general. It happened all too often. Stryker didn't like many officers. A lot of them achieved their rank based on politics or nepotism. They got quick promotions and held their rank for show and bragging rights. Capable officers often struggled to be promoted because they didn't play politics, but they did know how to win battles. One day, Stryker would become an officer. He would rise to the rank of major. He was not promoted to field grade officer from a captain's rank because of politics, nor because of his competency in battle. His superior officer, Colonel Wexler, supported Stryker's promotion because the colonel felt that if he didn't get the man promoted, Stryker would kill him.

Stryker rose from behind the tree and ran, hunching low, to the next big oak. When he heard Minshew coming up behind him, he took off again. They reached the corner of the house and rested to catch their wind.

From what Stryker could see, the house looked deserted. Weeds had overtaken the grounds. Even in dim light, he saw the spacious porch with its columns and railings had large patches of paint peelings. *I hope it's not too rundown for the general.*

In two or three more hours, it would be light. Returning to their unit in the day would be more dangerous. Stryker figured he and Minshew needed to secure the premises and get back to headquarters in the next two hours.

"Stryker, Hunnicutt, and Jenson are dead," Minshew whispered. "Could have been one of us."

"Say it say quick," Stryker hissed. Not yet nineteen but he was a callused sergeant, a non-commissioned officer with four hard-earned stripes on his sleeves, three up, one down. Four years of fighting will wring the boy out of a man.

Minshew had only been in the Army for three-and-half months. At age twenty-two, he was four years older than Stryker, but it didn't matter. Minshew took orders from the sergeant without questioning the young *non-com.* Minshew respected experience. He knew how Stryker fought with gun and blade.

"I only volunteered 'cause the war gonna be over soon, and I got paid fifteen hundred dollars to take another man's place, a rich man's son." Minshew paused, but only for a moment because of Stryker's obvious impatience. "I didn't think I was gonna be doing any real fighting."

"You're a soldier."

"I have to admit I'm not a brave man," Minshew said, shaking.

"None of us are."

"I've seen you in battle, Stryker. You don't look scared."

"Follow orders. Think about that."

That's how the Army trains a soldier. To not question orders.

"I don't wanna get killed doing this. I have a wife and a two-year-old boy."

"Do what I tell you."

Minshew took a deep breath. "What do I do now?"

"Stay off the road. Go around, right of the house. I'll go left. Meet in the back."

Minshew reluctantly nodded. He knew there was nothing else to be said. He duckwalked to the end of the porch and peeked around the corner. He rose to a crouch, glanced at Stryker, and disappeared around the house.

Stryker started across the front yard. The sky began to clear. A smattering of stars poked through open spaces, and the faint glow of a three-quarter moon showed behind a thin cloud. He was glad the rain had let up, and if the moon remained behind a cloud, that was fine with him. He rounded the left corner. Weeds grew two feet high along the side of the house. The place gave every appearance of desertion. Stryker relied on past experiences to remain vigilant. He had seen a lot of relaxed dead men. There were no lights inside the house. He caught sight of his shadow along the wall and crouched lower. The moon had broken free of cloud cover. *Need to get behind the house and out of the moonlight*, he thought. Stryker quickened his strides and rounded the rear corner. Minshew moved toward him. They met at the steps to the back door. Stryker led up the three steps and tried the door. It was locked.

A hard kick from Stryker's boot opened the door. He entered the veranda and waited for Minshew to come in behind him while his eyes adjusted. Moonlight cast an eerie glow on the four pieces of wicker furniture. He saw another door directly across the enclosure. Carrying the rifle ready, Stryker stepped to the second door. It was unlocked and he cracked it open. The kitchen. It was dimmer than the veranda, and again Stryker and Minshew took time for their eyes to adjust. A cooking aroma filled the room. Someone had recently been in the kitchen. Stryker slipped to another door opposite side to open it.

It led to the dining room. A white tablecloth lay on the six-foot table. Six chairs wrapped around the table and two plates, and two cups sat on the table. An open, arched doorway on the far side of the table led to an expansive living room. Stryker and Minshew eased around the table toward the doorway. There was a double-door entry on the left and a spiral staircase on Stryker's right. A large river stone fireplace, which was empty of fire, beyond the stairs. A door past the fireplace was open. Stryker thought it could be the study. A faint light showed from inside. Another door that was closed could have been to a bedroom.

Stryker turned to Minshew. "I'll check out the rooms down here," he whispered, pointing with the gun barrel. "You head up the stairs. Take it slow. I'll follow after I check these two rooms."

Holding the Spencer ready, Stryker crept past the staircase, glancing up at the empty steps and into the open room. The study was empty.

Stryker had just emerged from the study when he heard two gunshots. *I told him slow, dammit!*

Stryker resisted the urge to race up the stairs. Instead, he quick-stepped to the foot of the stairs, raised the rifle to his shoulder, and rested his forefinger on the trigger before placing a boot on the first step. He kept himself next to the wall and worked his way up the staircase. *Jensen and Hunnicutt would have been helpful here, but they fucked up. Just him and Minshew now, or maybe just him.* When he'd climbed halfway, he saw the glow of lantern light from an open door that belonged to the last room on the left. He reached the top of the stairs. On the way to the lit doorway, he passed two closed doors without opening them. An intricate wood railing ran along the balcony overlooking the downstairs. It went unappreciated by the young sergeant. He glanced behind him and then focused on the lit door.

Stryker heard nothing through the dimly lit doorway. Remaining close to the wall, Stryker edged to the open door. He poked the rifle barrel around the door jamb, peeked in the room, and pulled back. He had learned to make quick looks. Soldiers who lingered around corners often invited bullets. He saw Minshew curled up on the floor five feet inside the bedroom. A female stood by a bed.

Before Stryker peeked in the bedroom again, the woman said, "I knew there were more of you Yankees."

Keeping the rifle ready to fire, Stryker peered into the bedroom. She stood at the top of the bed on the far side of the room. She wore a pale green nightgown. She was medium height, thin, and wore her shoulder-length hair pinned back on one side. Stryker thought she was attractive, but didn't dwell on it. He was on a mission and needed to stay alive. Too many times, he had seen a soldier let his guard down, and it cost him his life. An elderly man with white hair and a long white beard lay with his head on a blood-soaked pillow. There was a bullet hole in his forehead.

Stryker scanned the room and then asked, "Anyone else in here?"

"No."

"In the house." Even at his young age, Neville sometimes asked questions in a statement.

"Just me and my daddy, who's dead." The woman pointed at Minshew on the floor. "He shot him."

Stryker closed the door behind him. While holding the rifle pointed at the woman, he stepped to the other side of the doorway so that if the door opened, he would stand behind it. He pointed the gun at Dokes.

"Your daddy shot Minshew?" Stryker noticed the revolver in her father's hand.

"Yes."

"See if Minshew's still alive."

The woman was slow to move.

"I can shoot you and check myself."

Taking slow, hesitant steps and with a careful eye on Stryker, she walked to Minshew and knelt on both knees. She laid two fingers on his neck. "He's alive."

Minshew mumbled a few words, too low for Stryker to make out what he said.

"What'd he say?" Stryker kept the gun on her.

She placed her hand on the floor for balance, leaned down, and put an ear by Minshew's mouth. "Say it again."

Minshew whispered. He was growing weaker.

The woman straightened. Still on her knees. She looked up at Stryker. "He said, 'I kept off the road'."

Minshew's body went slack. She felt the side of his neck again. Held her fingers there for three long seconds. "He's dead."

"Show me around. I want to make sure you're not lying about no one else here."

The woman got to her feet. Saying nothing, she walked to the closet and opened the door. She swung out her arm, inviting Stryker to look inside.

Stryker stood behind her and he shoved her into the closet with the rifle barrel. The small enclosure was dark. Too dark to see well.

"Get the lantern." Stryker backed out of the closet. Watching her come out and while keeping the gun trained on her, he asked, "What's your name?"

"Verity."

"Verity, bring it over here." Stryker flattened his back against the wall next to the closet door. He kept his finger on the trigger. He watched Verity to ensure she picked up the lantern and not the handgun.

Verity returned with the lamp.

She held it up shoulder-high and entered the closet.

Stryker swung around to stand in the doorway. Clothes hung on three racks, men's suits, slacks, and shirts on a single wooden rod. There were dresses, blouses, and skirts on the other two bars.

"Hold the lantern low and pass it around under the clothing," Stryker said.

Verity bent down with the lamp at one corner so Stryker could see if there were any legs underneath. She shuffled around the closet, holding the lantern near the floor, and stood up at the fourth corner. "There," she huffed. "You see, there's no one hiding in there."

"Take me around the rest of the house." Stryker doubted Verity and her daddy were the only two people in the large house. Together, they went through all the rooms, upstairs and downstairs, including the basement. Finally, after Stryker had Verity show him the rest of the house, and upon finding no one else, they stopped by the fireplace downstairs. The search took a half-hour.

Stryker's uniform remained wet and muddy, especially the front, and his body shook from the chill and the strain. Two men had been killed by snipers and a third by an old man. No matter how many deaths he'd seen, they still affected the young sergeant. He was also tired from lack of sleep and needed a break.

"Build a fire, Verity." Stryker took off the muddy coat and plopped down in a chair by the fireplace.

Verity cast him a scornful glance and gathered papers and kindling. Stryker watched how she placed paper and kindling on the grate in the firebox, crumpling the paper, crisscrossing the small sticks, and meticulously preparing a fire like a surgeon preparing for surgery. He wondered why she had not asked to change out of her nightgown. She struck a match on the stone hearth, lit the paper, and straightened to gaze at the nascent flame. The fire caught, and Verity carefully put two pieces of cut and split logs atop the kindling.

Satisfied with the fire, Verity turned to Stryker. "Anything else?"

Stryker would have liked a hot cup of coffee, but he did not want her out of his sight, and he was not about to get up and follow her into the kitchen. "No." He wondered why she hadn't cried or shown remorse over her daddy's death.

"You look young to be a soldier and a sergeant," Verity said, standing between Stryker and the fire. "Shavetail, how old are you, fifteen?"

"I'm going on twenty," Neville replied with indignation. "I'm a sergeant, not a lieutenant." Second lieutenants are called shavetails by subordinates in the Army, indicating their inexperience. The derogatory term came from untrained horses who had their tails shortened. It is the term lower ranks used for young troopers of any rank. Fresh-faced lieutenants received the most usage.

Verity shrugged her shoulders and sat in the chair next to Stryker's. He adjusted the rifle on her. "Christ, shavetail, you don't need to keep pointing that damn gun at me. I'm through with this fucking war."

Stryker let the barrel drop a little to the side, so it was not aimed directly at her. He had never heard a refined southern belle cuss like she did. Even though she only wore a nightgown, she looked elegant to Stryker. He figured she must mean what she said. He kept his eyes on her, anyway.

Verity, who had been watching the fire burn, must have felt Stryker staring at her. She turned to face him. "I lost my husband three years ago up north. I don't know where he was killed. Don't know where he's buried. Two brothers were killed too. And for the life of me, I don't know why we're still going about killing each other."

"Slavery," Stryker offered, and then immediately regretted saying it.

"Shit, shavetail. I know that. You think I'm stupid?"

"Stop calling me shavetail! My name's Neville." Stryker pointed the gun at her again.

Verity repositioned herself in the chair to face Stryker. "What I am saying is, couldn't we have figured out how to end it without killing six or seven hundred thousand of us? Stupid? I'll tell you who is stupid!" Verity's voice was elevated. "The fucking bastards who started this God-damned war!" She nodded violently with each word. "The cotton gin is replacing the need for people to pick cotton." Then Verity turned it down a notch. Having made her view of the war clear, she sat back in the chair. "God in Heaven," she huffed, looking up at the ceiling.

Stryker had not thought about the war like Verity said. He didn't know what to say.

"How did you get in that uniform?" she asked.

"You mean in the Army?"

"Don't tell me you volunteered."

"No. I got conscripted."

"Jesus, they must be desperate."

"I'm old enough."

"Old enough to die, I guess, and you won't even understand why."

Stryker had not thought that much about it. One day, soldiers arrived and got him out of school, gave him a uniform and a rifle, and told him it was his duty. Sitting there with Verity, he figured she was way beyond him in reasoning things out. He kept quiet. He already felt foolish enough in front of her.

"Neville, you know why my daddy was up there in that bed?"

She called him Neville. He liked that. Liked how she said it. A strange feeling ran through him. He sat up in the chair and turned to face the woman. She still looked at the ceiling. He studied her profile; she had a straight chin, delicate high cheekbones, a small, pointed nose, and a smooth elegant neck. A few stray strands of hair lay across a finely curved forehead. Young Neville had yet to learn how to properly appraise a beautiful woman. However, in the small hours of the morning, in the middle of a savage war, Neville Stryker was about to get a lesson.

"I hit him with a skillet," Verity recounted with her eyes closed. "Yep, hit him in the head with an iron skillet."

"What for?"

Still talking with closed eyes, Verity continued. "We had been married six years, my husband, Joshua, and me. Six good years before he went off in this damn war. He didn't have to. He could've gotten out of it. He went 'cause he said it was the honorable thing to do." Verity released an exasperated breath. "Honorable," she repeated. "Southern boys fought for honor, huh… now Jesus H. Christ." Verity opened her eyes and looked at Stryker. "What are you fighting for, shavetail?"

"I told you not to call me that." Stryker was disappointed she returned to shavetail, but he kept the gun off her.

Verity closed her eyes. "Why did I clobber Daddy? I'll tell you. He said since I wasn't being tended to…" Verity opened her eyes and looked straight at Stryker. "That's what he called it, tended to. He was drunk. I guess that was part of it." She sat back and closed her eyes again. Maybe having her eyes closed made it easier to talk about it. "That he, my own father, would tend to my needs. He came up behind me in the kitchen, grabbed me up here." Verity bounced both hands off her breasts. "And that's when I hit him with the skillet."

"Shit!" Stryker exclaimed, under his breath. He hadn't known anyone who committed incest. Heard about it. He just never knew anyone who did it.

"That's why you didn't cry."

"What's that, you say?" Verity sat up, turned to Stryker.

"I wondered why you weren't more upset about your daddy."

Verity settled back in the chair. She kept her eyes open. "Maybe I shouldn't have hit him. Mother has been dead a long time." Verity sat up again and stared at Stryker. "But it's just not right. It is not right at all."

"I don't think it is." *That was fucking brilliant, shavetail,* Stryker said to himself. He struggled to come up with something that didn't sound dumb.

Verity had Stryker locked onto her now. She had his full attention. She furrowed her eyebrows and bit her lower lip. The woman looked like she was wrestling with something. Her facial features loosened. Whatever was bothering her, she'd made up her mind about it.

Neville, have you ever been with a girl, a woman?"

"Well, I—"

"Don't lie. Please do not lie. You'll ruin it."

"No, ma'am." Stryker suddenly felt he had to be honest with her. No idea why. She held him with a steady glare that stripped the bullshit out of him.

"Good. I want the last time to be with a virgin."

Stryker chewed on what Verity meant by "the last time" as she slipped from the chair and knelt between his knees.

She gazed up at Stryker. "Undo your pants."

He fumbled with the rifle, trying to decide what to do with it. *Would she try to grab the gun?*

"Never mind. I'll do it. Hold on to your gun."

Stryker felt a little foolish holding the rifle as Verity unbuttoned his Army-issued wool trousers. At least he didn't have it pointed at her.

She undid the last button and felt inside the wool pants for his penis. It jumped when her fingers touched it. He was getting hard fast, and she had to struggle a bit to get it out of his pants.

Verity gently stroked the shaft while looking up at him.

Jesus, that feels... "Why, Verity? I'm a Yankee." He felt a little guilty. He'd fought in Pennsylvania. Could have killed her husband for all he knew.

"Not by choice. You told me that. Besides, you're here. I'm here. It's four in the morning. You wanna leave?"

Stryker couldn't say yes with her stroking his dick[1]. So, he said, "No."

"Good, let's go into the bedroom down here and lock the door. Take off those muddy pants. Do not leave your gun out here." Verity pulled Stryker up from the chair by his penis. She grabbed the lantern and led him to the bedroom while hanging on to his rigid member. Stryker followed. Verity had a strong grip.

She kicked the door closed behind them, let go of him, and locked the door. "Take off those filthy clothes. If it makes you more comfortable, you can lie on the bed away from the door with your gun near you on the floor. I'll lay closer to the door." Verity set the lantern on the nightstand.

Stryker suspected the bedroom was for overnight guests. The closet door hung open with no clothing inside. The furniture was sparse yet accommodating: a king bed, two stuffed chairs with a lantern on an open nightstand table. Books filled a bookshelf cabinet at the foot of the bed. A wash basin was set atop a cherry-wood cabinet beside the bookshelf. Large area rugs covered much of the polished oak flooring. Two more lanterns hung on green wallpapered walls. The bed was a spindle, four-poster king, made of dark wood. Stryker had no interest in guessing what kind.

Stryker finally got his clothes off–he had taken extra time trying to decide whether he should get fully undressed. Once he saw Verity turn down the covers and get into bed naked, he figured it out.

"Just lay beside me for right now. You'll need to be taught a few things, Neville." Verity patted the bed beside her.

Bashful, yes. Awkward, yes. But Stryker had a sizable erection. That must account for something. He slipped beside Verity.

"Hold on," Verity said, as she sprung from the bed. "Stay right there. I'm just gonna get a wet towel and clean you up a bit." She took quick little steps to the wash basin.

Stryker leaned over the bed and reached for the gun.

---

1. Yep, "dick" came into usage for "penis" in the 1880s by the U.S. military

"Neville!" Verity saw him sitting up with the gun. "We're past that," she scolded.

Verity returned with two towels, one wet and one dry. She held them in front of her breasts, covering them. The dark triangle below her stomach was uncovered. He had never seen a woman down there and couldn't help staring. She saw him looking and smiled. *It was so natural for her.* No way could he understand how this was happening, and he had difficulty comprehending it. Her father? How was she ignoring his death? All of it didn't make sense to Stryker. For now, though, he regretted grabbing the rifle. He laid it back on the floor.

Verity bathed him, including his private parts, and then toweled him off. It was a lesson in cleanliness he would carry with him into the future. When she finished, Verity lay down beside him. "Now kiss me."

Stryker rose onto his elbow and bent to kiss her lips.

She pulled away. "Not like that. Don't purse your lips like you just ate a raw persimmon. Relax 'em. Now kiss me again."

He kissed Verity full on her mouth, this time without pursing his lips. Her lips felt soft and yielding. *She was kissing back!* He could feel her gentle breathing through her nose as they kissed. *She seemed so willing!* His body shook. He had a tingling in the small of his back. He couldn't stop the shaking. *Shit. Embarrassing.*

What Stryker did not know was that his exhilaration brought Verity to a higher level of excitement as well. Finally, she pulled her mouth away.

"Now, I am going to lie here with my eyes shut. Run your fingertips around my breasts, squeeze them gently, pinch the nipples sometimes, not too hard, and pull on them a little. Just do that for now. Another time, and for another woman, use a silk scarf or a feather. The idea is to tease me, play with me, and take your time. Please a woman, Neville, and she'll please you." Verity closed her eyes.

Stryker, remaining on his elbow, hesitated, taking a moment to study her slender body. Soaking in the female form. He had not seen a woman nude before. Her breasts were firm, not particularly big, and with perky, extended nipples. Flat stomach, bony hips. The dark patch.

Slender legs stretched out. A beautiful woman was lying next to him, telling him how to make love to her, wanting him. He was nervous. *Shit, can I please her?* While he thought about things, Verity began gently stroking his penis.

Nerves be damned. Stryker moved his hand to one of the soft mounds and started dancing his fingers around her breast. He caressed both breasts drawing circles around them with his fingertips. Then he tried pinching and tugging on a nipple between his thumb and forefinger. He thought he heard Verity release a low moan. Glancing at her face, he couldn't tell. Acting out a hunch, he leaned closer and kissed her, like she taught him. She gave him a little smile. Her eyes remained closed; the kind of smile that suggested he had learned how to do it. He tugged on the second nipple. Both the little nubs now protruded out a bit more. *Fascinating.*

"Stryker, take your time and start running your fingers down my body, slowly." She tugged on his penis to make her point. "Tease me."

Stryker was beginning to get the hang of it. He danced his fingers close to her pubic area four times and then retreated up to her breasts. He ran fingers along her ribs, and she told him it tickled. "I like it though," she said.

"Use your hand and nudge my thighs apart, gently."

He nudged. She helped a little.

"Now run your fingers inside of my thighs, tease me, but don't touch higher yet." Her hand continued slowly stroking his penis.

A bit frustrated, Stryker wondered when they were going to get to the fucking part.

"Tickle the hairs."

He used a forefinger.

"Now pay attention. At the top of my vagina, there is a little nub. Find it."

He stuck his finger inside, feeling around.

"Not inside. Outside at the top." Verity waited for Stryker to find her clitoris. "That's it. Stryker, that little nub is the most sensitive part of a woman's body. It's called a clitoris. Massaging it helps arouse a woman and makes her wet inside. Be very gentle at first."

Lightly touching, he ran his finger around the little nub.

"Lick your fingers and go back to what you're doing. I want to watch you lick your fingers."

Stryker and Verity looked at each other as he wet his fingers.

"I'm wet inside now. Put your fingers in me."

Stryker dipped two fingers in her. She was very wet. He withdrew his fingers and caressed her clitoris. The groan was unmistakable. Verity was undulating her hips now, rubbing herself against Stryker's fingers. "Does that feel good?" he asked sincerely, naively, but sincerely.

Until this time in young Stryker's life, he thought sex was for the sole pleasure of the male, that it did not feel good for the female, it might even hurt. That was why the girls he knew did not want it. Boys were always talking about it. The boys must have liked it. No one ever told him girls did, too.

Verity's answer to Stryker's question was an orgasm. It started with a low guttural groan from within and rose to come out her mouth as a higher pitched, "Oh, God!" She grabbed his hand and held it as she completed her climax. He tried to keep moving his fingers. She held tighter to stop him. When she finished, she relaxed her grip and encouraged him to continue by moving his hand in a slow, circular motion on her clitoris. Verity had another one.

For the first time in his life, Stryker knew he could pleasure a girl, to a woman. He liked that. He liked it very much. From that moment on, and for the rest of his life, he would take immense delight in pleasing a woman.

Verity had a third one. Then she took his hand and pulled him up to her. "Kneel next to me up here." When he did, Verity got up on an elbow and took his penis into her mouth.

Baffled, and fascinated, Stryker watched Verity suck on him. She worked her lips and tongue around the head of his dick, and then up and down the shaft. He got over that bafflement in a hurry. He closed his eyes and threw back his head. It felt so damned good. Just when he thought he might explode, Verity stopped.

"Now you do me. Down there," she said.

"Do what?" Stryker cursed himself for asking, but it was only fair. He didn't know what she meant. He twisted around and scooted down between her legs with his head facing her feet.

"Put your hands under my butt and lift my hips a little."

Stryker placed his palms under her and lifted.

"Now use your tongue on me."

With her hips now raised, it made her clitoris more accessible. *Okay, that is what she wants.* He began to lick it. To his surprise, she tasted sort of sweet. He heard Verity moan.

"Kiss it with your lips and lick at the same time."

Stryker did as he was instructed. She jerked her hips around, making it difficult to keep his mouth on the clitoris.

"Now, Neville," Verity's breaths were coming fast. "Feel up inside me with a finger. Up top, there is a little round spot that feels a little rough. Rub it. Gently." Verity was telling Stryker about the Gräfenberg spot, the G-spot.

Stryker did as he was told, and Verity had another orgasm, a good one.

"Okay, Stryker. Now, fuck me."

No problem getting in. Verity was sopping wet. Once in her, he knew what to do. He moved in and out, slow at first, and then faster.

"If you feel you're gonna come, stop and grind deep inside me, bite a lip, pinch your fingers. Think about the pain. I don't want you to come too soon."

Stryker had to bite and pinch himself two times, but he held off. Verity used her hand on herself and kept having orgasms.

"Wanna come?" Verity did not have to ask twice.

They did it missionary style. They did it with Verity on top, straddling Stryker. They did it with Verity on all fours, dog style. They did on their sides, both sides. He came three times. They rested a bit, and he came once more with a little effort. If Stryker had not been an eighteen-year-old with a pocket full of hard-ons, he might not have survived.

Finally, after three and a half hours, they had enough. They lay side by side on the bed.

"You can do other things to build up to it," Verity said. Use your imagination. Play a game. My husband and I used to play strip poker with cards. The loser of each hand had to take something off. When all clothes were off, the loser had to do sixty seconds of slavery." She paused and then added, "Live through this damn war, Neville. Get married. Have a good life. You gonna make some woman very happy."

Stryker got a good education that night.

It was getting light outside when Stryker walked out the front door. Verity had already climbed up the stairs to her father's bedroom.

He was about to close the door when he heard the gunshot. A single shot, nothing more.

"The last time, with a virgin." Stryker finally understood. The chilled realization ran through him. He closed the door. There was no need to go upstairs.

The morning sun poked through the clouds and shined on the road and on the blue uniforms of Stryker's unit marching toward the house. The snipers must have moved off. No shots came from the trees.

CHAPTER SEVEN

Of all the deaths in that damn war, Verity's punched the hardest. He was young. Life is bigger when you're young, especially with the first girl. Not until Leigh and her death, did Verity, and how she died, fade. Leigh's death trumped Verity's. It was the worst loss and always would be.

The fireplace fire in the Hopkins parlor had died down. The rain outside dwindled to a light sprinkle. Stryker sat in the wingback, recollecting until he heard the pipe organ playing upstairs. He should have inspected the house earlier, he chided himself. Had to be another person, or persons, in the mansion. The two men he had killed were in no condition to be at the organ. He doubted they could ever play the instrument. They did not look like the types.

Stryker rose from the chair. He pulled the Peacemaker and stepped quietly across the living room floor to the massive staircase. The grandfather clock in the vestibule chimed two o'clock, startling him. *Have I been here that long?* "That organ playing must have had me imagining shit," he murmured. Nevertheless, he was running out of time if he were to keep his appointments. It was not a good idea for the police to know he'd made an earlier visit to the mansion. The two dead men made it messy. He decided to check on the pipe organ and leave.

The stairs ascended to an open mezzanine overlooking the parlor. The staircase railing continued across the mezzanine front as a safety barrier. The music grew louder as Stryker neared the top of the stairs. He stepped onto the mezzanine floor and saw another stairway leading to the third floor. Constructed with dark lathed woodwork and brass, the huge pipe organ was built into the wall overlooking the parlor.

Stryker eased to the edge of the mezzanine, and as he peeked around the wall, the music stopped. The organ bench was empty. He stepped out from behind the wall. The room sat vacant except for two rows of eight straight-back wooden chairs, arranged in an arc facing a piano in the corner. The mezzanine was the music room. If there had been more comfortable seating before the massacres, it must have been moved by the owner or stolen. An eight-foot-high glass-colored window on the far wall allowed light in the room. Bare hardware on the three walls showed where artwork used to hang. A door on the abutting wall by the piano was closed. He stepped to the door and opened it. A narrow wooden staircase led to the fourth level. Stryker closed the door and turned his attention to the pipe organ. He placed his hand on the padded bench and found it still warm. *Ghost butts do not warm benches.*

Planning to make a thorough search of the house later, Stryker holstered the Colt. Whoever played the organ had left through the small stairwell. He would climb those stairs when he returned. For now, he needed to get out of the house. He went back down to the parlor, took the stairs to the first floor, and then down to the basement. He stepped over Rafer's body and went out the basement door. He climbed up the steps outside and left the Hopkins mansion.

Striding down the hill to catch the cable car, Stryker figured he'd learned a couple of things inside the house. The two men in prison either had help if they participated in the murders, or more likely, they had nothing to do with them. He felt sure the two burglars he had killed were not part of the Hopkins's murders either. Second, whoever else was running around in the house played the organ.

It neared three o'clock when Stryker entered the Palace Hotel's lobby. The lobby was crowded with guests checking in. Other hotel guests lounged about the opulent interior. In front of the archway to the carriage turnaround, a docent stood by seven-foot potted ferns and was giving a talk on the Palace's history. A front desk attaché noticed Stryker as he made his way to the check-in counter. The clerk angled a nod to Stryker's right and behind him. Stryker tracked his gaze past three young men talking to three young women and saw two policemen in high-back chairs staring at him. They got to their feet as he approached.

"Mister Stryker," the taller of the two said, as he extended a handshake. "We're to escort you to the jail." He noticed Stryker's hand flash to the butt of the Peacemaker. "To interview two prisoners," he quickly added.

"Any news on the murders?" Stryker politely asked.

"No, nothing," the tall one said. "Since we have the killers in jail, no new happenings at the mansion either." The shorter policeman nodded.

Stryker figured interviewing the two men in jail to be a waste of time. He was convinced they were not part of the murders. Still, he went along with the policemen's presumptions, thinking it was not a good idea to let them know he had just come from the mansion. The police officers were friendly enough. Stryker deemed most of the young police officers were amiable. The young ones naively processed the law as best they knew how. It was when they rose in rank that maintaining their positions sometimes became more important than administering the laws. These two freshly scrubbed officers displayed no ranks on their sleeves, indicating they were junior grade and just on escort duty. No use priming them for information; they wouldn't know anything. "All right, fellas. Take me to jail."

"Yes, sir," both answered at the same time. The short policeman stepped aside, allowing his taller partner and Stryker to walk together, weaving through guests to the carriage roundabout. A police carriage with a single horse was parked at the opposite curb. Drivers of the jostling horse cabs pulled up to let the two police officers and Stryker walk between them. They viewed the three men with serious, yet quizzical expressions since the tall man with the police officers was not wearing handcuffs, and he *was* allowed to carry his gun.

The three rode in the buggy; the two policemen sat on the driver's bench in front. Stryker sat alone in the back. Drizzling rain continued to fall, bringing with it fog that shrouded the tops of buildings. No one talked. Stryker mulled over what he planned to ask the jailed men he was to meet. He doubted they had little to add to what they had already told the police. Nevertheless, he would go through with the interview. You never know. He gazed out the side of the buggy and saw buildings he had not noticed before. New streetlights lit recently constructed buildings, two- and three-story brick houses. Every time he left San Francisco and returned, the city left him further behind. It was no wonder that people shot him more strange looks lately. His well-worn denims and the Peacemaker were not particularly stylish in the present-day city. People in the city seemed to be trying to see who could be the most up-to-date, wear the newest styles, and be the biggest snob. *Ah, fuck it.* He settled back in the seat. *Why the hell would someone play the organ while I was there in the Hopkins mansion?*

The police buggy stopped at the foot of Telegraph Hill on the corner of Broadway and Romolo Place. The Broadway Jail was a solidly built two-story, stone structure. The entrance was at the top of a flight of stairs that ran up the front wall. The jail could hold 180 prisoners and had an enclosed yard in the back. It's unknown how many prisoners have escaped, but twenty-four were executed before its destruction in the 1906 earthquake. Some prisoners escaped during the quake.

The policemen hopped from the buggy. The short one stood by the carriage step, holding the door open. He extended a hand to help Stryker step from the buggy. He quickly withdrew it. The officers led Stryker up the stairs to the front doors of the jail.

The entrance opened to a thirty-foot paneled hallway with three closed doors on the left. A waist-high counter ran halfway down the right. Heavy iron bars with open slots for mail and small items topped the counter. Five policemen were seated behind desks in the open room on the other side of the counter. The door to that room was at the far end of the counter. At the end of the hallway, a door made of iron bars opened to the two levels of prisoner cells. A heavy metal chain with a sturdy lock hung about the bars. It served as added security to the lock in the door.

"Mister Stryker is here to interview the Bosworth murderers," the tall policeman said to a sergeant standing behind the counter. The sergeant, whose name tag read, "Odell," eyed Stryker and growled, "Got to leave his gun here."

Stryker unbuckled his gun belt and slid it and the Peacemaker under the bars to the sergeant.

"Ralph," Odell called over his shoulder. "Take him back." The sergeant ran his finger down a cell block sheet. "Number twelve on the second floor."

Ralph, seated at the first desk back of Odell opened a drawer and pulled out a hefty brass key ring with multiple keys. He came out into the hall eyeing Stryker with none-too-friendly eyes. "Come with me."

Stryker followed Ralph down the hall to the cell block door and waited as he unlocked the locks and swung the door open. Once they were in the cell block, Ralph bolted the locks, and turned to Stryker, "Mister, if you're up to something, I guarantee you won't make it out of here."

"Just want to talk to 'em."

Ralph started up a metal flight of stairs on the right. Stryker followed him up to the second floor, and then down the steel grated floor by the cells. Inmates watched them walk by with silent stares. Halfway down the row of cells, they passed under a heavy cross beam overhead. Directly under it, on the floor, was a hinged platform. Had Stryker looked up at the crossbeam, he would have seen the rope.

Invited guests watched the hangings on the first floor while seated in two rows of chairs on an elevated stand. It was a hot ticket in San Francisco.

Ralph came to cell number twelve and unlocked the door. He waited for Stryker to enter and relocked it. Ralph lingered in front of the cell until Stryker turned and glared at him, and then he walked where Stryker couldn't see him.

The two men lying on the double bunks hardly stirred. They had to have heard the cell door open and close. Stryker had spent time in jail more than once. He hated it. Hearing the cell door slam shut the first time is something a person never forgets, and one never gets used to it either.

The cell was eight feet deep and six feet wide. Two bunks and a toilet bowl with no seat were the only furniture. It was the men's home until the hanging. They must see the rope when going to eat. There comes a time when all seems lost, when there is no hope, and when a person gives up. Nothing to do but lie on a bunk.

Stryker felt no kinship with the jailed men. They were robbers or at least intended to rob. He despised thieves. To him, a thief deserved a death sentence. He had conducted those sentences himself more than once. Those who robbed him never got a second chance.

Stryker pulled the sai. Stepped to the inmate on the bottom bunk. His eyes were closed, and he failed to see the weapon that got jammed between his teeth. The long center tine pricked the back of the man's throat, and his eyes flashed open.

"Augh!" The inmate grabbed Stryker's wrist and tried to pull the tine from his mouth. Stryker pressed his shoulder against the sai's pommel and kept the tine jabbed in the man's throat.

"Hey! What's going on down there?" The top bunk mate leaned over the edge of his bed, saw Stryker, and yelled, "Get off him!" He swung off the bunk and ripped at Stryker's arm.

"Back off, or I'll kill him," Stryker snarled.

The bunkmate tugged harder, ignoring Stryker's warning.

Stryker pushed in a quarter inch and withdrew the sai. He flipped it around and thumped bunk mate's forehead with the pommel.

"What's going on here?" Ralph yelled, running back to the cell.

The inmate with a lump on his forehead lay stunned on the floor. His cellmate sat up in the bunk, spitting blood. He tried to talk, but the blood drowned his words.

"We're discussing the murders," Stryker replied, turning to face Officer Ralph.

Ralph made an easy decision. He knew about the slaughter at the mansion, that a family, including a woman and two children, were brutally slashed to death. If those two men in the cell, had done it, and he thought they had, then they deserved what they were getting. Ralph turned on his heel and strode to the end of the walkway, pulling out a cigarette to smoke.

Stryker returned to the interview. The two men were about five feet, seven inches tall; they were dark-skinned, had long black hair, and three-inch beards. They both looked to be in their midtwenties. The man on the floor regained his senses and sat up with his back to the wall and his feet splayed out. He chose to stay seated on the floor and keep a low profile. Stryker grabbed the front of the bleeder's shirt, pulled him from the bunk, and shoved him down next to his cellmate.

"I have questions," Stryker said. "A powerful politician thinks you did not kill that family." Stryker let that sink in before he continued. "I'd just soon see you hang. But if you didn't murder the Bosworth family, we want to find out who did. If you can provide us with information to catch the killers, it might save your lives."

"What kind of information you want, mister?" the man with the knot on his head asked. He grimaced when he pressed on it. "Couldn't you have just asked first?" He spoke with an accent Stryker didn't recognize.

"Could've," Stryker drawled. "Don't like thieves. Tell me what you saw and heard in the house." Stryker reached behind him, grabbed a pillow from the bed, and pulled off the pillowcase. He tossed it to the bleeding inmate. "Wipe your mouth. You need to talk too."

"Me and Badrick went in the house through the basement. We didn't go there to rob the place."

The inmate beside him nodded as he bled on the pillowcase.

That was news to Stryker. "What were you doing in the house?"

"To kidnap the kids. But we wasn't gonna hurt 'em! An' we didn't kill nobody!"

"That right?" Stryker asked the bleeder.

Badrick pulled the pillowcase from his mouth. "Adio's tellin' you true." His accent matched Adio's.

"Hold them for ransom," Stryker said, assuming that was their plan. "How much money?"

"No money," Adio said, shaking his head. He dropped his eyes to stare at the floor.

"No money," Stryker repeated. "Then for what?"

Adio glanced at Badrick. "We was just told to grab the kids and bring 'em to a house down at the end of Townsend Street."

"By the pier," Stryker said.

Both men nodded. "Yeah," Adio said, looking down at the floor again.

Stryker figured that meant the children were to be held on board a ship. "Who told you to do it?"

Adio continued doing the talking. "A man down at the yard."

Badrick's bleeding slowed. Stryker figured he had swallowed enough blood to where he might get sick to his stomach. *I shouldn't have stuck him so hard*, Stryker thought. *Need him talking too.*

"Yard," Stryker repeated.

"Yeah, by the dry docks down at the wharf."

"Name. Describe him."

"Said his name was Remo. That right, Badrick?" Adio asked his cellmate.

"Remo," Badrick bubbled out the name and nodded.

"Tell me about him," Stryker demanded.

"We only met him twice, mister. Gave us twenty dollars apiece. Said he'd give us two hundred more when we brought him the kids."

"A piece," Stryker guessed.

"Yes," both men answered together.

"Said you met him twice. The second time was after you left the house with the dead family inside?"

"Yeah," Adio replied.

"Wha'd he say when you told him about the murders?"

"Nothin' he just walked off."

"You tell the police about Remo?"

"They didn't believe us," said Adio, shaking his head.

"You see or hear anybody else in the house?"

"No. Heard a door slam somewhere. That's all."

Badrick took the pillowcase away from his mouth. He wasn't bleeding as much now.

"Tell me the position of the family members when you saw them in the kitchen."

"The man and woman were tied up in chairs, blood all over their fronts and on the floor. Their heads were down but you could tell their throats had been cut. The two kids laying on the floor in front of 'em with throats cut too. Lots of blood on the floor. Awful sight."

"We'd never do somethin' like that was done to them people, mister," Badrick added.

Stryker leaned forward. He believed the two would-be thieves. The sincerity somehow seeped through. Nevertheless, he would still kill them if it were left to him. It became apparent, the parents watched their children killed, maybe tortured before their deaths. *For what purpose? Whoever killed that family was a special breed of evil motherfuckers.* If Stryker thought for sure the two men in front of him committed the murders, he would make sure they were hanged.

"Did you see anyone outside the house when you left?"

"No," Adio answered. But I think somebody saw us. The police said we was seen leaving the house before the bodies got found."

"If you hadn't gone there to kidnap those kids, you wouldn't be in this mess." Stryker rubbed the men's noses in their own shit.

"Yeah, we know," Badrick lamented. He looked like he was gonna cry.

"One more thing. Did you hear a piano or organ playing?"

The two men shook their heads.

Stryker turned and stepped to the front of the cell. "Guard!"

Ralph heard the call and came over. "You finished wit' 'em?" He eyed the two men on the floor. "You can have more time if you want it."

"Finished for now."

Ralph unlocked the cell door and stepped back for Stryker to come out.

Stryker had not learned much. He did think, like Hearst, that the two men didn't commit the murders–*what made Hearst think they didn't?* And that the family was being coerced to do something. Could be Samual Jonas was right about his suspicions about the new railroad IPO. As far as Stryker knew, the unions had not murdered women and children. They had threatened violence, but not that. Still, he needed to follow the leads, and union involvement was the only one he had.

The same two police officers who took him to the jail brought Stryker back to the Palace Hotel. They accompanied him into the lobby and waited in a corner while Stryker went to the front desk.

Hotel Attaché Willard rushed to greet Stryker and hand him an envelope. Stryker opened it and stepped away from the front desk, allowing other guests to take his place while he read it.

Stryker, I want you to spend tonight in the house. The police commissioner said he would send two men with you. Also, I arranged lanterns for you. Thanks, George.

Stryker crowded back up to the front desk. He was not in the best of moods. *Pushing it, George.* "Got lanterns for me?" he asked Willard.

"Oh, my gosh! Yes, sir. Just a moment." The attaché stooped behind the desk and straightened holding two kerosene lanterns. He set them on the countertop and bent down again for the third one.

"Hold them for me. I'll get them after dinner." Stryker noticed the police officers waiting for him in the corner and motioned to them. They met halfway across the floor.

"You two taking me to the mansion?"

"Yes, sir," the tall one replied smartly. He straightened, got a salute halfway to his brow, and then dropped it. His shorter partner straightened too. Both appeared ready for duty.

"A couple hours before dark," Stryker told them. "Let's eat dinner first." He spun around and headed for the men's grill.

The two young officers looked at one another. They arched their eyebrows and shrugged their shoulders. "He did say, 'Let's,' Lawwill," the tall policeman said.

"Then, *let's* go with him."

"Three for dinner," Stryker told the grill room maître D who was wearing a black tuxedo.

Eyeing Stryker and the officers behind him, the maître D executed a short bow, and said, "Right this way, gentlemen."

They were seated at a booth. The policemen took off their caps and placed them between each other. Stryker kept the Stetson on.

Once settled in their seats, but before receiving menus, Stryker spoke about the night ahead. He sat on one side of the table. The officers sat opposite him. "We'll search the house first," Stryker began. "There may be hidden passageways. If so, we need to find them." Stryker glanced up at the waiter approaching their table. "Shit."

The waiter, wearing a short-waisted, white mess jacket and maroon slacks, placed the menus in front of the three men. He asked for drink choices and all three chose coffee. The waiter then recounted the specials, spun on his heels, and left.

Stryker noticed the officers glanced at one another and he figured they were having trouble reading the menu since so many items were in French. "Just order a steak and tell the waiter how you want it."

"Yes, sir. Nolan and me don't know French," Lawwill said, sounding apologetic.

"They put food choices in French so they can charge more. Get potatoes and a vegetable with the steak."

"You two been to the Hopkins mansion before," Stryker asked in a statement.

"Er, no sir," Lawwill stumbled a reply. It took him a bit to realize he had been asked a question. "Detective Stiner and three more officers, one by the name of Jarvis went to investigate the place. I don't know the other two men who went with him."

Nolan was looking around, surveying the room while Lawwill talked. Stryker guessed neither of the two officers had dined in the Palace Hotel before. Lawwill and Nolan could have been brothers, Stryker thought. They both had jet-black hair, dark eyes, and sharp features. Lawwill was at least two inches taller, though. Stryker didn't care enough to ask about it. "You talk to Stiner or Jarvis about what they saw."

Lawwill was quicker this time. "I spoke to Jarvis. He said they searched all around the house but couldn't find anything." He elbowed his partner. "Nolan?"

"Uh, no." Nolan swung his attention back to Stryker. "I never talked to 'em, but the neighbors said they heard voices coming from the house, loud voices during the night, a man and woman. Scared 'em they said." Nolan glanced at Lawwill." You knew about that, right, Lawwill?"

Lawwill nodded.

"Any officers there at night?" Stryker asked, this time.

"Don't think so." Lawwill turned to Nolan, who shook his head.

Stryker chose not to bring it up then, but he was puzzled why whoever committed the murders might remain in the house. *Looking for something? And why the voices? Why not just be quiet about it, and look for what they are trying to find? If... that is, they are searching for something. Trying to scare people off? The niece? While they look? Maybe. Still doesn't make sense. Is something else going on besides the IPO? Might not even be about that. Need to ask a ghost.*

"Tonight, if we find someone in the house, don't kill them unless you must. I want to talk to 'em," Stryker said. "Whoever did the killings, hid, or disposed of the bodies. The dead are either still in the house or taken out without being seen, maybe through a hidden door or passageway."

The waiter returned with a silver coffeepot and porcelain cups on a rolling tray. After filling the cups and serving the coffee, he took food orders, steaks for all, medium cooked, and potatoes and beans to accompany the main course.

Stryker waited until the waiter left to pick up where he left off. "Search the house thoroughly." He tried the coffee. It was not as strong as he liked, but it would do. He was used to trail coffee that had to be strained through his teeth. Stryker remembered the men he had killed in the mansion earlier that day, Rafer and his thieving pal. These two policemen will see them in the house, dead with neck wounds. "No telling what we might find."

Not much else was said between Stryker and the police officers before the arrival of *filet mignon and pommes de terre*. Each man kept to his thoughts while dining. Other than coffee cups refilled by the waiter, the men ate their meals uninterrupted.

When finished, the waiter returned and asked, "Mister Stryker, will there be anything else?"

"No." Stryker never ate dessert.

"Then have a pleasant evening, sir." The waiter submitted a short bow and walked away.

"Stryker got to his feet. "Let's go."

"What about the check?" Lawwill asked, rising from the table.

"No check." Stryker exited the grill room.

Lawwill and Nolan looked at each other, arched their eyebrows, and then followed Stryker. They made a quick stop at the check-in desk for the lanterns. Each took one and they continued across the lobby toward the front doors.

Outside, they waited for the Market Street cable car and rode it to the corner of Market and Powell. There they caught the Powell Street cable car up to the Mark Hopkins mansion on Nob Hill. Horse cabs did not go up Nob Hill. The Powell Street grade was too steep at 25%. Too many horses got injured on the hills in San Francisco. It was the reason Andrew Smith Hallidie invented the San Francisco cable system–to save the horses.

Lawwill used a skeleton key on the Mortise lock to unlock the massive double doors. Hearst said he would provide a key; Stryker supposed he meant a skeleton key. The grand entrance opened to the second floor. Stryker and the officers paused to light the lanterns in the vestibule and walked into the parlor. The mansion was updated to have electricity, but the power had been turned off. Hearst must have already known it and that's why he provided the lanterns. Earlier in the day when Stryker had visited the mansion, he entered through the basement and not through the vestibule and reception room. He recognized the parlor, though. It was the expansive room with the built-in fireplace where he had sat and built a fire after killing the robbers. Holding the lantern higher, the glow illuminated the built-in, magnificent grandfather clock. Dutch paintings hung on a wall. The double-height ceiling added a dramatic feel. The entire room had intricately carved first and second-grade dark walnut. Around the corner from the parlor's entrance hallway was a bifurcated grand staircase. The intricately carved stair hall led up to a two-story mezzanine arcade and the twelve-foot, built-in pipe organ. High above the staircase, the frescoed ceiling framed a large skylight. The parlor had two chairs in front of the fireplace and three island pedestal cushions aligned in the center of the room. No other furniture sat on the walnut-planked floor.

"We'll start in this room. A secret passageway is more likely to be on the ground level," Stryker said. "Spread out and run your hands over the walls, feel for cracks, a door, knock on the walls for a hollow sound. I'll search on this wall behind me. You do that one and that one." Stryker swung the lantern toward the wall across from him and then the one on his right.

The three men separated to feel the walls. Stryker heard the two officers rapping on the wood with their knuckles. When they held the lanterns in front of their bodies, he saw their black looming shadows by the walls. Across from the fireplace the wall had no windows. It was load-bearing support. Still, there could be a hidden doorway that might lead to outside. Stryker suspected if there were hidden passageways they would not be in the parlor, the room they now searched, nevertheless he wanted every inch of the mansion examined, and he figured they had to start somewhere. As Stryker ran his hands along the walls, he regretted not procuring the services of a professional builder who would be more adept at finding hidden doors or tunnels. He and the police officers were amateurs, probably wasting their time. *Shit.* The crude inspection took twenty minutes. When finished and finding nothing, they rejoined at the fireplace.

"You two stay here. Do the wall around and under the staircase. I'll go to the kitchen and Hopkin's office." Stryker figured officers Lawwill and Nolan would discover the door to the basement. He also surmised they would not venture down to the basement without him. Although they hadn't received instructions from their superiors to follow Stryker's orders, the two young policemen obeyed. He watched them carry their lanterns to the staircase and then he went to the office.

Deep russet wood panels covered the walls. Two thick Persian rugs covered much of the finely polished flooring. Another fireplace, smaller than the one in the parlor was positioned in the room, and there was a massive mahogany desk with a leather wingback chair. A floor-length window was behind the desk. Bookshelves filled with leather-bound books lined one of the walls. Stryker figured they were for looks. No one reads that stuff. Finding no clues or anything suspicious, he left the office and walked through the dining room to the kitchen where he expected to find the dead burglar on the floor.

He pushed through the swinging door. It was dark, very dark, and he turned up the lantern and held it higher to illuminate the room. The lamp base cast a large round shadow on the tile, and he canted the lantern to shed more light on the floor.

No dead body. Stryker held the lantern shoulder-high in front of himself. He walked around the entire kitchen. Nothing. The dead thief couldn't have somehow crawled away. He saw no blood on the tile, nor could he see any other sign of the killing. Someone went to the trouble of removing the body and cleaning up the mess. Why? The dead man, Rafer, in the basement, had his body been moved, too? *What the hell is going on in this damn house?*

Stryker continued searching around the kitchen. After ten minutes, he gave up and went back to the parlor to meet Lawwill and Nolan by the fireplace.

"We found a door under the staircase," Officer Lawwill told Stryker. "There is a set of stairs going down to a lower level."

"Probably to the first floor," said Stryker. "Let's go on down to the basement." The first floor could wait. The rooms on the second floor, like the solarium, and a bathroom, could wait too. He wanted to get to the basement. Stryker moved ahead of Lawwill and led the officers down the stairs to the first floor and then on down to the basement.

Rafer's body was gone, gone like the other body in the kitchen.

Stryker stood where he had last seen Rafer's body, trying to guess why the hell someone had moved both bodies and cleaned up their messes.

Nolan, who was still by the basement stairs, suddenly yelled in a muffled voice, "Someone's playing the pipe organ!"

Stryker ran to the stairs. The swift dash blew out his lamp and he rushed up the stairs in the dark, taking two at a time. Lawwill and Nolan ran close behind while trying to their lamps lit. Stryker raced ahead using the staircase handrail as a guide. Clamoring up the stairs, their boots pounded on the bare wooden steps. Only when Stryker got to the second level did he realize they had made enough noise climbing the stairs, that the organ player would have heard them coming. The music stopped when he reached the parlor. *Shit.*

Lawwill bumped into Stryker in the doorway. "It's stopped," Stryker hissed. "I made too much noise running here." He blamed himself even though six boots were stomping up the stairs. It was something he practiced as a military commander. Don't blame your men for failures on the battlefield. Blaming them is how an officer loses respect.

Stryker relit his lantern and the three of them continued up the grand staircase to the mezzanine. Of course, they found no one, and it was not apparent where the organ player had disappeared to, or how he had accomplished the feat. One thing the men knew, they were not alone in the mansion.

"What do you want to do now, sir?" Officer Lawwill asked.

"Let's see what we can find up here," Stryker replied.

"Why do all these mansions have pipe organs?" Nolan asked. "Makes it eerie when they play 'em," he said, anxiously looking around the room.

None of this makes sense, Stryker thought. Body snatching, music playing, what could be accomplished by it? They found another staircase behind a closed door.

"A person could have gone up the stairs," Stryker said. "Could have been smart enough not to stomp his boots."

"You want us to go check out the stairs, Stryker?" Lawwill dropped the *sir.*

"Go ahead."

The two officers drew their police-issued revolvers, held up the lanterns, and entered the staircase, stepping quietly up the steps.

Stryker strolled around the room, running his hands along the walls, looking for hollow panels, or hidden doorways. Somehow, whoever is in here can come and go and take bodies from the house without being seen. There was no decomposition stench so the dead were either buried outside or taken somewhere. They could be spirited away from the mansion. *Spirited, by spirits*. Stryker's hand drifted down to the Peacemaker. The police who had conducted searches had not found anything. Nolan was right, the mansion was a creepy place. Stryker thought the.44 could handle things.

"He doesn't want us to shoot unless we have to. Bullshit," groused Officer Nolan, in a whispered rant. "I'm shootin' first. If they're still alive, he can ask 'em whatever the fuck he wants."

"Just don't shoot me," Lawwill rasped.

"Place gives me the creeps."

Lawwill was three steps from the top of the stairs when Nolan touched his back. "Let's stop a minute and listen."

"Relax, a little, dammit," Officer Lawwill cursed. "You're creeping me out with your shit talk." He brushed Nolan's hand away. "Besides, nothing could be scarier than that son of a bitch downstairs. His fuckin' face and *his* ghost eyes. That's what gives me the creeps. If Death had eyes, they'd look like his. C'mon, let's check out the next room and go back down." Lawwill started up the stairs again.

"All right," Nolan grumbled as he followed. "But to tell the truth, I feel safer with him than with you."

"Fuck you."

Lawwill and Nolan reached the top of the staircase and stepped onto the fourth floor. They came out into a hallway that led around to the mansion's tower, the highest point in San Francisco[1]. Four bedrooms branched off from the hall. The rooms were smaller than those on the lower floors. Ornate windows on the north and south sides

---

1. Eadweard Muybridge shot his famous panoramic photograph of the city atop the open-aired, railed roof.

had gables. The east and west windows were plain and rectangular with no gables.

The officers had taken ten steps down the hallway when Lawwill holstered his handgun and grabbed Nolan's arm. "Shhh! Listen!" he whispered.

"I don't hear—"

"Shush." Lawwill squeezed Nolan's arm tighter. "Don't you hear that?"

"Yeah, now I hear it," Nolan whispered back. "A woman? Humming?"

"Sounds like it." Lawwill pulled his revolver again. "Down the hall, round the corner," he rasped. They crept farther down the hallway, lanterns out and guns cocked. Coming to a corner in the narrow hallway, they stopped to listen again. The humming was louder.

"I think it's coming from inside that door down there," Lawwill whispered, pointing his gun toward the third door down the left side of the hall. "I'll stay on this side of the door. You get on the other side. Try the doorknob. Crack it open."

"Don't you think we oughta go back and get Stryker?" Nolan whispered. "Could be more than just her in there, Lawwill."

"C'mon," Officer Lawwill growled.

"I don't have a good feeling about this, Lawwill. Hold it." Officer Nolan used the hand holding the lantern to grab Lawwill's shoulder. The hot lamp rested against his partner's shirt.

"Ouch, dammit! You're burning my back!" Lawwill hissed.

Nolan pulled his hand back. "Listen, maybe the humming is to get us up here and they're waitin' to shoot us when we open the door."

Nolan's warning caused Lawwill to hesitate. Only for a moment, though, then he managed to shake it off. "Okay, Nolan, you stay here. I'll open the fucking door." Lawwill's foul language helped him gin up the courage. He took three more steps down the dark hallway and paused.

Lawwill looked back at Nolan who was waiting. *Damn, Nolan.* Since Lawwill flaunted his bravado, false or not, he had to uphold it. *Shit.* He tightened his grip on the revolver. "Can't go back for Stryker now. That fuckin' Nolan," he cursed under his breath. Officer Lawwill moved very slowly and very quietly to the third door.

When Lawwill got within a few feet of the third door, a floorboard creaked under his shoe. *Ah, for God's sake.* He flattened against the wall and waited. He heard nothing. Nothing included the woman in the room. She'd stopped humming.

Lawwill glanced behind him. Nolan was still standing in the hall, watching. He hadn't taken off down the stairs. Good. Lawwill waved his arm with the revolver in an angry "C'mon" motion to Nolan. He hoped Nolan saw it.

Officer Nolan slowly crept down the hallway and Lawwill huffed out "Thank you, Jesus," under his breath. He faced forward again and took a short step, carefully easing his foot down to full weight. No creak. *Good.* Three more cautious steps and Lawwill reached the room. He heard nothing. He crossed to the other side of the door and waited for Nolan.

Nolan stopped at the door. He looked at Lawwill, watching for his next move.

Lawwill held out his lantern for Nolan to take it. It was then that Officer Lawwill realized whoever might be in the room could see the lamp light under the door. *Ah, shit.*

Lawwill placed his hand on the doorknob and turned it. He nudged the door open with the gun barrel and waited a moment. Nothing came from inside the room. Lawwill shoved the door hard. It swung open and banged against the wall.

Officer Lawwill fired three quick shots into the room. He stepped back, flattening himself against the wall, breathing hard. "They shot at me!"

"I think it was the door, Lawwill," Nolan hissed. He was breathing hard too. "Did you see something?"

"No. You think it was the door?"

"Yeah, it banged against the wall when you shoved it."

"Fuck."

"I hear Stryker running up the stairs."

Stryker reached the top of the stairwell, stopped, and held out his lantern. He couldn't see the policemen. He drew the Peacemaker and started down the hallway. He rounded the hall curve and saw the two officers standing by a door. The one closest to Stryker held two lanterns. He could only see the shadow of the second officer. Both were alive, not doing anything but standing there.

Stryker lowered his lamp and walked down the hall. No need to be stealthy, now. He strode next to Nolan. "What's going on?"

"We opened a door." Nolan tried to indicate which door by clumsily pointing with the two lanterns. He lowered the lamps instead and said "This one. We thought we heard a woman humming in the room."

"Who fired the shots?"

"I did," Officer Lawwill said. "Didn't mean to."

"Didn't mean to." Stryker edged around Officer Nolan to peek into the room.

"It sounded like a gunshot in there," Lawwill explained.

"The first shot was the door. There were only three shots," Officer Nolan supplied, standing behind Stryker.

The room was too dark to see anything. Stryker stepped back. "You see anything in there?" He directed the question to Officer Lawwill.

"No, didn't get a chance."

"Stryker, you and your trigger-happy cops gonna stand out there talking shit, or you are you gonna come in the room?" A woman asked.

She knows my name. Stryker tried to think where he had heard that voice, it sounded familiar. "You alone?" He was not about to walk into a room at the invitation of a woman and get shot.

"Yes, been waiting for you, Stryker."

"It's okay," Stryker said. He stepped through the doorway. The officers followed, figuring Stryker must know the woman.

Stryker saw her sitting in a rocking chair. He held up the lantern to get a better look. "What are you doing here, Rawlings?"

"I came to talk to you," Rawlings said, rocking her chair.

"You could have spoken up earlier," Stryker said, moving closer. Lawwill and Nolan remained behind Stryker.

"Saw you here earlier in the day. Didn't know where you stood until you came in with those two fellows behind you," Rawlings said, with a grin. "Then I decided the police spoke well enough for your character."

"Puts you on the same side," Stryker drawled.

Officers Lawwill and Nolan kept silent.

"Suppose." Rawlings rested a .38 revolver on her lap.

From what Stryker could see in the dim light, she wore a black suit underneath her dark wool waistcoat. Her blouse, or shirt, was also black, buttoned up to her neck. Her black fedora was cocked to one side of her head, completing the masculine ensemble. *Why is she dressed like a man*? Stryker wondered.

"Want to tell me who you are, what you do, and then fuck me to death?" Stryker asked as he drew up a chair from the writing desk. He spun it around and straddled it with his arms crossed on the chairback.

Her laugh was easy.

Stryker remembered Rawlings from the saloon and thought at the time she was kind of attractive when she smiled. He thought Rawlings couldn't be her real name.

"I can tell you some of what I do," Rawlings replied. "I can only reveal a bit; I don't know who *you* work for, and why *you're* here. You'll have to tell me what you're looking for." Rawlings glanced past Stryker and eyed the two police officers. "Then there's those two chaps behind you. My job is top secret." She let that sink in and then continued. "My superiors are in Washington. Of course, I cannot reveal who they are, just that they are high up," Rawlings clipped. She spoke like a government agent, direct, assertive, and condescending. "What I tell you must remain between you three. I thought of sending the officers out of the room, but then they would report I was here anyway. So, gentlemen, I shall speak to all three of you, take you under my confidence, and rely on you to keep quiet about what I am about to tell you—for the good of the country."

Stryker twisted around in his chair. "If any of this gets out, you will lose your jobs and go to prison." He faced Rawlings. "I can do that. I'm supposing you can too. Their names are Officer Nolan and Officer Lawwill."

"That's why I feel I can speak somewhat freely with you tonight," Rawlings spoke directly to the two officers. "You must understand, you will be punished severely if you blab about me and what you hear." Then she turned to Stryker. "I can also do that to you, Stryker, although I wouldn't want to."

"Don't threaten me, darlin'. Might lose my temper." Stryker did not suffer threats well. His pale eyes narrowed.

There was silence for a spell. Rawlings, Lawwill, and Nolan's lack of response suggested they believed Stryker.

"I believe I can trust the two policemen," Rawlings countered, seeking to defuse the tension. Rawlings then appraised Stryker's worn denims and the low-slung Peacemaker on his hip. "You don't look like a police officer, Stryker. I'll chance it."

"We can be trusted," Officer Lawwill said.

"Absolutely," Officer Nolan affirmed.

Stryker said nothing.

"Good," Rawlings announced. "I am a government agent, here to investigate a subversive group." The tension in the room waned, but not entirely because Stryker's stark warning still lingered. "We have received reports this group is operating here in San Francisco."

Officers Lawwill and Nolan edged closer.

The lamplight shined brighter on Rawlings's face. She did seem a bit more relaxed. She paused for questions or comments and got neither, so she continued. "These people are breakaway anarchist radicals from the Socialist Labor Party of America."

"And somehow connected with this place," Stryker suggested.

"We think so. Bosworth participated in a railroad initial public offering the unions and this group was against."

"They killed the whole family for that?" Officer Lawwill asked, incredulously.

"Perhaps not the sole reason." Rawlings stopped rocking and leaned forward in the chair. "Bosworth was a wealthy man." She leaned back and did not resume the rocking. "Somewhere in the house, there is a safe. We think there is a lot of money in it. Additionally, names and addresses of would-be wealthy investors in the stock offering could be found in it."

"How do you know that?" Officer Nolan asked.

"Bosworth's partners suspect that is where he kept his money and securities. They were not in the office or at the bank where he banked, and he confided with one of the partners that he had a safe at home. Someone must have let that information about the safe and what was in it slip. Mary Hopkins, Mark's widow, cleaned it out before she left for Massachusetts. So, what's in it is Bosworth's. We learned that much from Mister Jonas, Bosworth's brokerage partner.

"You don't know where it is." Stryker sat the lantern on the floor. Scooted it with his foot toward Rawlings to shed more light on her and get the lamp smoke away from him.

"No."

"Mrs. Hopkins," Stryker suggested.

"Mary Hopkins is extremely ill. She wants nothing to do with the mansion. In fact, her current husband, architect Edward Searles, whom she married last year, drew up plans for the construction and he won't let anyone talk to her."

"Searles, her new husband, how about the scandal?"

"You know about it?" Rawlings acted surprised Stryker knew about Mary's quick association and marriage to a man everyone thought was after the Hopkins fortune.

"In the papers."

"Yes, I suppose it made quite a splash."

The policemen let Rawlings and Stryker do the talking.

"The Bosworth niece," Stryker said. "She's on her way to San Francisco."

Rawlings arched her eyebrows. Cocked her head. "Correct, Stryker. But you didn't read that in the papers." She wanted to ask him how he came to know that privileged information, but she held off.

"You suspect she might know the whereabouts of the hidden safe."

Rawlings nodded. "Main reason why she's coming, don't you think?"

"Don't know the girl. Maybe she's righteous."

Rawlings produced a halfhearted laugh. "Maybe, I guess. Anyway, we hope to find out when she arrives. It is her money, and we need to safeguard it for her and keep the private investor names out of anarchist's hands.

"So, you're staying here to see if the anarchists return?" Officer Lawwill interrupted.

"As much I can. The police do not think it is worth their time. They don't believe the radical gang knows about the safe or what's in it. I disagree and so do my superiors," Rawlings answered.

"But you know they do," Stryker said.

"Yes. I can't tell you how."

"An undercover man," Nolan blurted. "You've got an undercover agent with them."

Rawlings said nothing.

Stryker had suspected as much. Kept it to himself.

"Has any of them showed up?" Officer Lawwill asked.

"I thought two of them had. Turns out those two were just trying to burglarize the place." Rawlings directed her response at Stryker.

"And…" Stryker held her gaze.

"Murdered like the Bosworth's. Throats cut."

"Holy shit!" Officer Nolan turned back to the door, rubbing his throat.

"We weren't told about that," Lawwill said.

"I left to get the police. When I returned with two officers and a detective, the bodies were gone. They would not even draft a report. They thought I made up the killings." Rawlings stared at Stryker.

"I believe you," Stryker deadpanned. *Why is she not telling I killed 'em?*

"I heard them talking before they were killed," Rawlings supplied. "They were not anarchists. And I despise thieves too."

"That's how she knows," thought Stryker.

"I am sure the anarchists returned while I was gone. Disposed of the bodies as they did with the Bosworth bodies. For the life of me, I cannot figure how, Stryker."

"No bodies, no investigation." Stryker supplied.

"Yes, but still, *how* remains a mystery." Rawlings returned the deadpan.

"This place is haunted," offered Officer Nolan.

"Swacker Brothers, the contractor who built this place is supposed to have the blueprints ready for me tomorrow. That damn Searles, the architect, won't help."

"To look for hidden doors, passageways," Stryker said.

"How long do you and the officers plan to remain here, tonight?"

"All night. We haven't finished searching the house."

"All right, I'll leave. Let you finish your search. Listen for Mark," Rawlings said, and she laughed. It sounded like a passing remark, a light addendum.

"Mark," Stryker repeated.

"Oh yes, surely, you have heard. The mansion is haunted."

"Haunted?" Officers Lawwill and Nolan exclaimed together.

"Haunted by Mark Hopkins and others too, I guess," Rawlings replied, saying it like it was common knowledge. She continued to astound the officers. "Mark Hopkins didn't live to see the mansion finished. Everyone knows he was building this monstrous house for his wife, Mary. She was the one who wanted it. And then, after Mark died, she immediately took up with Searles, the architect, to live in the mansion. Ol' Mark must have turned over in his grave. Perhaps, he even got out of it," Rawlings said with a smile.

"You've seen him?" Officer Nolan asked, his voice two octaves higher.

"No, just heard him."

"You heard him?" Officer Lawwill asked incredulously. He had to have been on his toes. His words were elevated too.

Stryker listened impassively.

"I have. Heard a woman or a girl crying, too." Rawlings had the two policemen on a string now. She was enjoying it. "Mark wanders about these halls calling for his wife, yelling, 'Maaareee! Maaareee!'"

"Tell me about the woman or girl," Stryker said. But he figured Rawlings was the woman doing the crying.

"Soft crying, not loud wailing, just quiet-like. I thought it came from one of the upstairs rooms, but I never found her."

"Weren't you scared?" Officer Nolan asked.

"Yes."

"She's just kidding," Officer Lawwill said dryly.

"Actually, I'm not," Rawlings said stoically. "I'll leave you three brave men here in the mansion and I'll get some sleep." With that Rawlings picked up her satchel and rose from the rocker.

"If you have trouble getting the plans, tell the contractor, Senator Hearst sent you to get them," Stryker told her.

"George Hearst? You know him?" Rawlings asked. "I mean you know him that well?"

"I'm staying at the Palace Hotel. Should be back later tonight. If necessary, contact the senator for his approval at the hotel. Use my name. You get the plans; I will go with you to help with the search. Ask for me at the front desk."

"There are many mysteries here," Rawlings said.

Officers Lawwill and Nolan remained silent.

CHAPTER EIGHT

Stryker watched Rawlings exit the room and listened to her footsteps go down the hallway. He then spoke to the two policemen, "Let's go find ghosts. Start on this floor. Find the door that leads to the rooftop." Stryker picked up the lantern and led them from the room. The rocking chair no longer rocked.

He held the lamp higher to go down the corridor. Officers Lawwill and Nolan followed. The paneled hallway was narrow, only five feet wide. The men walked single file. Officer Nolan brought up the rear. Stryker tried two doors that opened to bedrooms before he found one that opened to a set of stairs leading to the roof. Officer Lawwill and Officer Nolan trailed behind Stryker. Nolan closed the door before starting up the stairs. No one spoke.

At the top of the stairs, the steps creaked under each boot. Stryker opened the door to the roof. A rush of fresh air struck his face, almost blowing out the lantern. A strong wind swirled the fog around the tower. He shielded the globe with his hand from the wind and surveyed the twelve-by-twelve roof. A four-foot-high latticed iron railing ran around the edges, guarding against a person from accidentally stepping off the roof. He also found a metal fire escape ladder which reached the ground. It could have been used to leave the mansion. Stryker grabbed the ladder's handrail and tried it. It seemed solid enough. It would not have been easy to carry bodies down it, though. *Must be another way to haul bodies out without being seen,* Stryker reasoned. Still, the ladder was an alternate escape route. He spun on his heels and strode briskly to the roof door to get out of the wind and return to the fourth floor. Officers Lawwill and Nolan went with him. The two policemen, who were a little embarrassed by their actions outside Rawlings's room, followed quietly.

They inspected all the rooms on the fourth floor, including closets and bathrooms, and didn't find any hidden passageways, just two flights of stairs leading to the third floor. During the search, they heard no calls for Mary or a weeping girl. Stryker did not believe in ghosts. None had ever contacted him. Nor did he believe others who claimed they had seen spirits. Could there be an existence of some kind after death? He could not say. God? Stryker did think God existed, but as far as that relationship was concerned, he and God left each other alone. Nevertheless, Stryker was bitter over Leigh's gruesome death. She was an angel or was to Stryker. Had he been punished? Stryker certainly deserved it for his many killings, but couldn't he be punished without taking an innocent life? Her face and the way she looked at him as she lay dying in his arms, flashed through his mind. He tripped and almost fell. "Shit!"

"What is it, sir?" Officer Lawwill asked Stryker, descending the stairs behind him.

"Nothing," Stryker retorted, annoyed that the remembrance of his wife interfered with the present task at hand. It felt like weakness to him. *No, it is not a weakness,* he angrily scolded himself. Remembering Leigh is never a weakness. Stryker would not forget the way Leigh looked, happy, or dying. He couldn't, and besides, he didn't want to.

He came to the third floor and stepped out into the mezzanine. The organ bench was empty. So was the piano. They found nothing unusual in the room. Stryker even had them examine the organ and crawl up inside it. The hallways were wider and longer, and it took more time to bang on all the walls. The four bedrooms and two bathrooms required more time as well. They found nothing.

Stryker then led the officers to the first floor, skipping the second level they had previously searched. The northern end of the first floor had no natural light since it was constructed into the hillside. Stryker and the policemen took more time to examine that level. It was part of the ground level. During the hour-long search, Stryker only found one piece of evidence that caused his pause. They found a few drops of blood in one of the bathrooms. Nothing else, just four drops of blood near the sink. Whoever cleaned up could have been washing off the blood.

By the time Stryker and the officers completed the thorough, yet fruitless search of the mansion, the big built-in grandfather clock on the second floor struck four times. Weary and getting a little loopy from lack of sleep, the three men gave up for the night. They rested on the second level near the grand fireplace. The two wingback chairs sat in front of the stone hearth, but since Stryker remained standing, neither Officer Lawwill nor Nolan took a seat.

"I am heading back to the hotel to catch a couple of hours of sleep. You men can go." That's all Stryker said about their long night's effort. He placed his lantern on the fireplace mantel, headed through the foyer, and left through the mansion's front door.

Officer Lawwill waited until Stryker was out of earshot and grumbled to Nolan, "I guess we're finally finished with him. Let's get the hell out of this God-damned place."

"God-damned is right," Officer Nolan seconded.

Stryker arrived at the Palace Hotel at 4:35 AM. He stopped by the massive front desk to collect messages. There was only one, a status request from Hearst. *After a couple of hours of sleep, George.* Reading further, the note included an invitation for breakfast at nine.

He'd moved toward the rising room when the attaché said, "There was a woman in earlier asking about you."

Stryker knew who he meant.

"She wanted to know who you were and about your relationship with the senator."

"What you tell her?"

"We don't give out information about our guests, sir, but I did say you stayed with us from time to time," the young clerk replied politely. "I never told her anything about you and Senator Hearst."

"Ring me if she returns." Stryker figured Rawlings would be back later in the day. He wanted to accompany her to the mansion. Okay, he was curious about her too. It wasn't any kind of intimate kinship. The woman was shrouded in mystery. *Who did she work for*? She was certainly one tough girl. He admired her for that. Hearst would be interested in her assignment here as well. And the woman was on the right side. Stryker despised anarchists, especially Marxist militants. He wanted to help her. If she were to encounter any of those militants in the mansion, he wanted to be there to kill them.

Stryker crossed the empty lobby and boarded the elevator to the eighth floor. By the time he walked down the carpet to room *812,* he was ready to hit the bed. He never was able to sleep more than three or four hours at a time, especially since his time in the Army, and then, since Leigh's death, it became even more difficult to get a good night's sleep. Although the bad dreams did not happen every night, they still ruined his sleep since he often lay awake worrying about them. As tired as he was this morning, there was still a good chance he might not get enough rest. He didn't.

Stryker woke up three and a half hours later in a cold sweat. His teeth were clenched and his body muscles cramped. He rolled out of bed and got to his feet to work the muscles. It was his morning routine, like going to the bathroom, washing his face, or shaving and brushing his teeth. It was a maddening alarm clock. Afterward, he made his way to the bathroom. Used the toilet before turning on the light. It was daylight outside, but the foggy morning did not allow adequate light into the bathroom. He stood next to the sink and studied the man in the mirror.

The face staring back at him looked tired and drained. A good way to start the day. *Shit.* Red lines streaked the white surrounding the gray orbs. He blinked and rubbed his eyes. More white hairs at the temples this morning. A few peppered the beard now, too. Sharper bones protruded over his sunken cheeks. Need a big breakfast. He turned on the hot water, tore his eyes away from the mirror, and when the water warmed, he washed his face. The morning routine.

Stryker stepped off the rising room at two minutes till nine. Hearst was already in the men's grill room having coffee when Stryker joined him at the usual booth. A silver coffee pot sat on the table. Stryker filled the porcelain cup with the strong hot brew and took a sip. He placed the cup back on the saucer. "Mornin' George."

"Mornin' Stryker. You been over to the Hopkin's mansion?"

"Found nothing. Met a woman named Rawlings. Some kind of secret agent. Meeting her again later today. Should have building plans."

"I'm surprised the police hadn't used 'em already," Hearst grumbled. "Kate Bosworth, that niece I told you about, she's arriving tomorrow, a day early. Before the rail strike, I think."

Stryker lifted his cup and took another sip.

Hearst drank from his cup. The senator smacked his lips, showing his satisfaction. He used the back of his hand instead of a napkin to wipe his mouth. Having worked for years as a common laborer in the mines, Hearst was not of the gentile set. He made a fortune in the mines but had not read any etiquette books. Emily Post was only sixteen at the time and had yet to publish any of hers.

"About Morgan," Hearst began. If she's not delayed by the strike, should be getting back from South Dakota on Thursday or Friday, I reckon. I told you this week. Wasn't sure exactly what day."

Stryker nodded.

"I'll see what I can find out about this Rawlings woman," Hearst said. "Make sure she's on the right side." Hearst caught sight of the waiter coming to take their breakfast orders and leaned back from the linen-covered table.

"I suppose you would need to know more about her too." The senator could have been concerned about Stryker killing her. That was if she got on the wrong side of the man seated across the table from him. He felt the need to prevent a troublesome situation. Hearst had no firsthand knowledge of Stryker's violent tendencies, nevertheless, he had heard the rumors and read newspapers that talked about violence erupting in areas where Stryker was thought to be. The senator had the good sense not to ask questions.

The waiter brought steak and eggs and strong black coffee for both men. Just two of the things the men had in common. The senator was once rumored to have killed a man as well. They were tough men with hard lives. Similar in many ways, but Stryker had a higher body count.

Although Hearst never lost his wife as did Stryker, he had his share of hardships. Also, Stryker never worked for years down in the sweltering bowels of the earth digging rock as a dollar-a-day miner. They earned each other's respect. Stryker performed secretive, sensitive tasks for Hearst and the senator protected him.

Once breakfast arrived, their conversation ended. When Stryker finished his meal, he rose and left the grill room without a salutation. Hearst was not insulted. He knew Stryker was loyal. What better compliment than that from a man?

Stryker picked up the *San Francisco Examiner* from the front desk and returned to his room. He sat in the stuffed chair next to the window and read the paper. There were fifteen minutes when he dozed. He would forgive himself. He needed the snooze to be at his best later. Might mean staying alive.

An hour and a half passed, and Stryker heard the knock on his door. He picked up the paper from his lap and got to his feet. He threw the paper on the desktop as he answered the door.

It wasn't Morgan like he'd hoped, even though she wasn't expected today. Instead, it was Rawlings, and she had fixed herself up. No business suit. She wore a white blouse under a navy-blue waist jacket with brass buttons and a matching blue pants-skirt underneath. At the skirt top, was a delightfully narrow waist. Stryker had not noticed that before. Her hair swept back and parted European style on one side. It was a light brown color. He hadn't noted that either. She had a dusting of rouge on the cheeks and a thin stripping of pale, brick-red lipstick on the lips. Rawlings was not a prostitute, but she boldly, albeit stylishly, added color to an otherwise stern countenance. The woman was trying. Stryker was impressed.

"Come in." Stryker pulled the door open wider and stepped aside for her to enter.

"Thank you," Rawlings said, entering Stryker's room. She carried a lantern and had a black leather satchel slung on her shoulder. She eyed Stryker's room approvingly. "Nice. Top floor, too. Impressive."

The king-size dark, highly polished walnut bed frame sat in a meadow of green carpeting. There was a matching walnut desk and chair. An electric chandelier, desk lamp, and reading lamp lit the room. Rawlings took it all in. She did not need to use the bathroom where she could evaluate the toiletry accommodations.

"Have a seat." Stryker turned the wingback chair around for her. He grabbed the desk chair for himself.

"I thought it would be better if we talked in your room." Rawlings settled in the wingback and swung the satchel off her shoulder. She sat it on her lap and unbuckled the bag. "Swacker Brothers wouldn't let me take the blueprints, so I made these notes," Rawlings said, withdrawing what looked like three pieces of five-by-seven sheets of paper; it could have been four. The top sheet had writing on it. There were no sketches.

Rawlings pulled from the bottom. "This one describes a passageway on the third floor, where the organ is. It shows a doorway on the wall opposite the organ. I'm not sure but I think that entire wall is all bookshelves." She handed the slip of paper to Stryker and waited for him to complete reading her notes before pulling out another sheet.

"Okay, this describes an opening in the bathroom on the fourth floor, the top floor. There is a full-size cabinet door where the opening is shown on Swacker's drawings. So, it could be behind that." She handed the second sheet to Stryker and waited for him to read it.

"Back to the third floor," Rawlings said. She continued with an explanation. "Apparently, there is an opening, or possibly a passageway, behind the bookshelves."

"The third one." Rawlings separated the last two sheets of notes and handed one to Stryker. "Second floor. That's where the foyer is, parlor, dining room, kitchen, the fireplace where you sat." She spoke while he read. "If I'm not mistaken, there is an opening in the hallway. Could be behind the full-length mirror. Mark's office is on this floor. I would think the wall safe, which was not on the plans is in his office."

Stryker read quickly. He looked up from the notes and waited for Rawlings to tell him why she had kept the fourth note as the last one to show Stryker.

"This one is on the first floor in the hallway bathroom." She handed Stryker that note sheet. I have no idea where they are talking about. The plans just say 'Chute.'"

Stryker took his time reading the last note. There was only one short paragraph. He read it twice. He shook his head and handed all four sheets of notes back to Rawlings. "Let's find 'em."

"No police this time?"

"You want them?"

"No need." Rawlings put the notes back in the satchel before she rose from the chair.

Stryker grabbed the Stetson off the bedpost and lifted his gun belt with the holstered Peacemaker off the headboard. "You got one under that jacket?"

Rawlings flipped open her jacket flap, displaying a Smith & Wesson Model 3, four-inch barrel in a black leather shoulder harness. The woman had thus far maintained a business countenance with Stryker. He figured she knew how to use a gun. He was glad they were on the same side. Not because he was concerned about going up against her. Stryker felt comfortable enough with his skills. He just didn't relish killing a woman like Rawlings, one whom he was beginning to admire. Admiration was enough, though he briefly thought about her grinding it out on the king-sized bed. That's how a woman like her would want it, he figured, but he pushed those ruminations aside.

What Stryker didn't know was that Rawlings had glanced at the bed too, and she thought about getting a good pounding on it.

As they waited for the elevator Rawlings said, "These rising rooms fascinate me." She gleamed at the elevator that just arrived and then grinned as the gate slid open.

Stryker allowed Rawlings to step in first and then followed. "Oh!" she exclaimed when the elevator dropped. She tried to steady her feet and reached for Stryker instead of the handrail.

He grabbed her upper arm. It was thin but muscular. Their eyes met a moment before each turned away. Stryker released her arm.

"Thanks." Rawlings produced a nascent grin. She appeared embarrassed.

"Takes getting used to."

"You seemed used to them."

Other hotel guests entered the elevator when it stopped on each floor. The rising room grew more crowded. Stryker and Rawlings stood quietly the rest of the way to the lobby.

"Lobby," the elevator operator announced, and everyone, including Stryker and Rawlings, stepped from the elevator.

"Out the front. Cable car at the corner." Stryker gave a gentle push on Rawlings's back as they wove their way through the guests to the front door. Naturally, a drizzle greeted them outside.

Stryker and Rawlings waited ten minutes for the Market Street cable car and rode it to Powell Street where they got off. There they caught the Powell Street cable car up to Nob Hill. They stepped from the car on Pine Street and walked to the Mark Hopkins mansion. That is when Stryker realized he did not have the key. He forgot to get it from Nolan or Lawwill. Didn't matter, he suspected they would not have given it to him without authorization, and he would have to wait for it. Hearst might have had to help. He was about to tell Rawlings he didn't have the key when she unzipped a small side pocket on her satchel and pulled out the key. It was a large skeleton key, matching the one the policemen had used.

They walked without speaking up the stone driveway and Rawlings unlocked the massive front door. She entered first and he followed through the foyer to the parlor. Stryker grabbed the lantern off the fireplace mantel and lit it.

"Let's make sure no one else is here," Rawlings said quietly while lighting her lamp. The rainy day only allowed a faint light indoors. "First, the first floor, then search our way up to the roof." She waited for Stryker's input but got none. "Then we look for hidden doors."

Stryker strode to the first-floor stairs and flipped the light switch on the wall just in case. Nothing turned on. He held out the lantern and started down, listening to Rawlings's footfalls behind him. They separated upon reaching the bottom of the stairs. Rawlings took the bedrooms on the right, Stryker on the left, and then they met in the hall after looking in each room. Rawlings had drawn the Smith and Wesson and looked ready to use it. The walls held no paintings, no furniture in the hall or rooms. All were taken either by Mary who took the stuff with her when she moved to Massachusetts, or she had given it away, or it was stolen. No one could be hiding behind a chair. There weren't any. There were six bedrooms on the first floor, a common sitting area for guests to congregate, and a bathroom adjacent to the guest lounge room. Each room also had bathrooms that Stryker and Rawlings checked.

When they finished, Rawlings approached Stryker. "I want to look in the bathroom back there." She held out her lantern and started down the hall. "The chute. Let's find it."

Rawlings led the pair to the bathroom. It was a ten-foot-by-ten-foot room with a toilet, sink, a dresser with a padded bench, and wood-framed mirror. Stryker took the mirror from the wall. There was no sign of an opening. The black and white tiled floor offered no clues either.

"All right, we can come back later. We better check the rest of the house." Rawlings walked from the bathroom and went to the stairs. "Up to the roof," she said, as she started up the stairwell.

Rawlings had taken charge of the search. It was all right with Stryker. He figured she was better at it, and besides, she was on the government's payroll, not him. He tagged along with his lantern and the Peacemaker.

He had been listening for strange sounds as they searched but hadn't mentioned it to Rawlings. Guessed she was too. So far, though, he had heard no crying, thumping, or organ playing. Maybe there was another woman in the mansion besides her. He realized now that she had lured him and the policemen up to the room with her humming. *Why didn't she just announce herself? Why the mystery?* He'd ask her about that sometime.

On the roof, they saw no one. There was no evidence of anyone having been up there either. Stryker and Rawlings investigated the fourth floor too. They saw nothing and heard nothing.

"Bathroom cabinet," Rawlings recounted slowly. "I want to take a look while we're up here." She said it faster. "It is the one at the end of the hallway, I think. Not in a bedroom. The plans said cabinet." She was talking to herself. Stryker eavesdropped.

He followed Rawlings into the bathroom. It had a toilet, sink, mirror, bench for the ladies to primp, and a cabinet opposite the sink and toilet. Like the other bathrooms in the house, the flooring was black and white tiles.

Rawlings went straight to the wooden cabinet which was built flush with the wall and painted a pale green to match the walls. She grabbed the round brass knob and pulled open the cabinet door. "Oh," she exclaimed to herself. Rawlings stepped back to look at the shelves.

Stryker moved beside hers. Inside there were shelves of towels, soaps, rolls of toilet paper, and fragrance bottles of different shapes and sizes. The bottles sat on the bottom shelf and had a two-inch lip along the front edge to keep them from falling off and breaking on the tile. *To keep bottles from falling off?* Stryker knelt by the cabinet.

Halfway down the right vertical frame was a metal bolt. It wasn't noticeably big, it protruded only a half inch and painted the same color as the cabinet's wooden frame. An inch-long groove ran behind the bolt. A latch?

Stryker slid the latch backward. The cabinet and contents sprung open. It was spring-loaded; the shelves, heavily loaded with sundry items, opened up about a foot. Stryker swung the cabinet wider. There was the door.

"I'll be damned!" Rawlings exclaimed, careful to keep her exclamatory muted.

Stryker bent down and stepped through the five-foot doorway. It was dark and he held out the lantern. There was a low ceiling, less than five feet high. A narrow steel-graded walkway led to the right. He set his foot on it. It held. He started walking to see where it led.

Rawlings was close behind him with her lantern bumping against his butt. Stryker briefly wondered if the walkway would support both their weights. He said nothing about it, though. The ceiling slanted lower, and they had to bend down to walk the grate, especially the six-foot-three mixed breed.

The walkway led to a spiral staircase. It extended up to the roof and down to floors below.

"Can you believe this?" Rawlings whispered, her face was within inches of Stryker's rear end.

For a moment, Stryker wished his ass could talk. It remained silent, though. The stairwell creaked a bit when Stryker put his weight on it, but it seemed sturdy enough. He started down the curved staircase. Rawlings let him go down three steps before she tried it. Coming to the next landing, which Stryker figured to be on the third floor, he left the staircase to step out on another metal walkway. It led to a door. Stryker ran the lantern up and down the door, looking for a doorknob or latch. He couldn't find one.

"It must only open from the other side," Stryker said to Rawlings who came up next to him.

"Should be at the bookshelves," she supplied. "Phew! Smells awful in here."

Stryker noticed the offensive effluvium earlier; he hadn't mentioned it. He knew what it was.

"We go up." Stryker proceeded back along the narrow walkway to the spiral stairs.

"Why not down?" Rawlings took off after him. When Stryker failed to answer her, she reached forward and tugged on his sleeve.

"Stryker! Why not go lower, see if we can come out another passageway?" He stopped at the staircase.

"We go back up to the fourth floor," Stryker whispered. Follow me. Keep your gun ready."

His last instruction caused Rawlings to pause. "All right," she whispered.

Stryker pushed the cabinet door open using the barrel of the Peacemaker. He stepped out into the bathroom. Rawlings came out behind him. He grabbed her arm. Putting a forefinger to his lips, he whispered. "Listen."

"What?" I don't hear anybody," Rawlings whispered back.

"Not a person."

Then, Rawlings heard the thumping. It came from below on the second floor. "What do you think that is?" she asked.

"Blow out your lantern and set it down." Stryker blew down the globe on his lantern and placed it on the floor.

Rawlings did the same. She straightened and waited for Stryker's next move.

Outdoors, daylight waned. Low black clouds made for an early evening. In the mansion, furniture became shadows to stumble over. "Wait, let your eyes adjust," Stryker hissed. He waited fifteen seconds and edged to the top of the stairs. He pulled the Peacemaker and grabbed the handrail to help lighten footfalls. He started down the stairs. Rawlings followed. He couldn't hear her, but he sensed she was right behind him.

Stryker stopped at the bottom of the stairs and surveyed the third floor, the pipe organ, and the bookcase where Rawlings thought there was a hidden passageway. There was no one. He crept to the head of the stairs leading to the second floor, and that's when he heard people talking in addition to the pounding. It sounded like someone was striking the wall with a heavy tool. *They must have found the wall safe.*

"Stay up here," Stryker rasped to Rawlings. He had gone down five steps and realized she had ignored him. *Shit.* Now he would have to watch her. Keep her out of the way. If she got shot, it would be her damn fault.

Stryker took forty-five seconds to reach the bottom of the stairs. He stopped every two or three steps to listen and try to see what was going on. The hammering came from the office. Whoever was in it was using a sledgehammer to break the safe out of the wall. They had discovered the safe but did not have the means to open it.

Stryker stepped off the stairs. The hammering stopped. He turned back to Rawlings and raised a forefinger toward his mouth, signaling for her to be quiet.

The office was around the corner. He heard people talking but couldn't see them. More than one man was doing the talking, and at least one woman. Could be just the one woman since he only heard a single female's voice. He counted four different men's voices.

He could tell by their conversation they had gotten the safe out and were deciding how to get it out of the mansion. They were debating on whether to go to the basement or the downstairs bathroom. *The downstairs bathroom*? *The chute*? Stryker gripped the Peacemaker tighter. The basement won out. Two men came out of the office, carrying the heavy safe. Two more men and a woman followed them. Those two men and the woman carried pistols.

Stryker leveled the Peacemaker and shot the first man carrying the safe. The big.44 round hit him in the chest. Left center. The safe thudded to the floor.

The full weight of the safe pulled the second man down before he could let it go. He lost his balance and crashed forward onto the floor.

Stryker's second bullet caught the third thief in the mid-section. He raised his gun to fire, but it fell from his hand, and he stumbled rearward into the fourth man, behind him. The fourth man's gun discharged, sending another bullet into the stumbling man.

The woman, who was too startled to aim properly, managed to get off a shot, and the bullet thudded into the staircase. Stryker's third shot hit her in the gut. The bullet blasted out her lower back.

Rawlings tried to get around Stryker to use her gun. Instead, she bumped into him, causing his next shot to miss the fourth man.

Before Stryker could recover, the two unharmed thieves escaped down the stairs. Somehow Stryker kept from cursing at Rawlings.

Stryker checked on the male thieves he had shot. Both were dead.

The woman was still alive when Stryker and Rawlings got to her. She was trying to sit up but could only lift herself to one elbow. Blood pooled on the floor beneath her. It was black. He got her in the liver.

"Who killed the family?" Stryker figured the woman had little time left. He needed quick answers.

"I need a doctor." She coughed and groaned in pain.

"If you want to live, tell me who did it."

"Please."

"Tell me."

"Jace and Jude." The woman moaned out the names. "Didn't mean to kill the kids." Her head drooped.

"That them?" Stryker swung the Colt barrel toward the two dead men.

The woman lifted her head. "No."

"Why?" Rawlings wanted to know.

"For the working man."

"What's your name?" Rawlings asked. She knelt to place her hand behind the woman's back.

"Mary."

"Mary what?"

"Sorbitch. Please, get a doctor. Don't wanna die."

Stryker brought the Peacemaker up and pointed it at Mary's forehead and fired.

Bones and brains blasted out the back of Mary's head. She slid off Rawling's hand and collapsed to the floor.

Rawlings was shocked. She stared at the welted red hole in the center of Mary's head. "You said if she wanted to live, to tell who did the killings," Rawlings muttered.

"I didn't want her to live."

Rawlings tore her eyes away from Mary's headache to see Stryker stroll toward the stairs and watched as he calmly pulled four bullets from his gun belt and loaded them into the Colt's cylinder.

"God help us all," Rawlings whispered. A bulge in Mary's pocket caught her eye. She reached inside it and withdrew a crudely bound book titled, "The Communist Manifesto."

Stryker kept his gun ready and started down the stairs.

Rawlings followed, reluctantly, but she did follow him, unable to think of anything better to do. She was careful to stay three steps behind. *What, he didn't like her last name?*

They reached the bottom of the stairs.

"Stryker wait." Rawlings wrapped her hand around his upper arm. "I found a book on her, *The Communist Manifesto*. Does that mean anything to you?"

"Written by Karl Marx," Stryker answered. His attention focused on the first-floor hallway.

"You've read it?" Rawlings asked. She sounded disappointed.

"No."

"But you do know about it?" Rawlings asked.

"The girl had it, you said." Stryker turned to Rawlings.

"Found it in her pocket."

"Should have shot her three times."

Jace and Jude were not on the first floor. Stryker and Rawlings inspected all the rooms and then went on down to the basement. The two men were not in the basement either. At first, Stryker suspected they had exited the basement and escaped from the mansion. He thought that until he saw that the basement door was locked. Locked from the inside.

"They're still in here," Stryker said, looking around.

"How could they be?" Rawlings whispered.

"They must have come in the basement and locked the door behind them to keep anyone else from coming in the house behind them. But those two men, Jace and Jude, did not leave the house down here." Stryker turned to the stairs, studied them for a moment, then said, "I want to check that bathroom again, the one with a chute," he said, making quick strides to the stairs.

Rawlings ran after him. "So, you think they're not here now?" she asked, breathing hard to catch up.

Stryker rushed up the stairs, taking two at a time.

"I guess not," Rawlings mumbled to herself.

At the top of the stairs, Stryker ran down the hall to the bathroom, his boots ran a loud, hollow cadence on the wooden flooring. There was no need to be stealthy.

Rawlings walked to catch her breath. Stryker stomped on the floor tiles when she got to the bathroom.

"Should be hollow somewhere," Stryker said, stamping his boots in the center of the room.

Rawlings started stomping near the sink and toilet. Her boots were five sizes smaller than Stryker's size 12s; they made lighter thumps.

"Here, Stryker!" Rawlings yelled, continuing to thud her boots standing near the toilet.

Stryker stopped thumping and knelt to rap his knuckles on the tiles. He found the edges by listening to the hollow and solid resonations. He tried prying open the hollow section with his fingers. "No good." He sat back on his heels.

"Must be a trigger latch somewhere in here," Stryker allowed, standing up to look around the bathroom again.

Rawlings reached behind Stryker and pressed down on the toilet handle. The toilet flushed. "Just a thought," she said with a light chuckle.

Stryker saw nothing that resembled a latch, switch, or a knob that could be as a release mechanism. He stepped over to the toilet. He jiggled the toilet handle. Nothing. Then, instead of pressing down, he lifted the handle.

The tile section popped open. "Spring loaded," Stryker said.

CHAPTER NINE

"Well, I'll be damned!" Rawlings exclaimed. "Look at that." She knelt to peer into the tunnel. "Where do you suppose it goes?"

Stryker lit a match and dropped it down the black hole. "No fat ghosts escaped through this," Stryker mused. "About three feet wide." The match flame went out after falling six feet. "Not sure, Rawlings. Drops straight down for a ways."

"I don't want you to go down that hole," Rawlings said as she took Stryker's hand. It was not a forceful grasp, implying a demand, or an act of desperation. She held his hand gently, caressing the leathery skin on the back of his hand. "Stay here with me."

Sufficient light showed in the bathroom for Stryker to see her face. The normally sharp-cut features looked less stern. Stryker met her gaze. She had a little smile.

Can it be that this stern-assed woman has become aroused by the preceding violence, the killings? To the mixed breed, that was not a flaw in her character. Endorphins can be released by more than one activity and then used for other things, pleasurable things, and it is not for him to question how that works. The woman had her blood running hot. A romp in the sheets with a woman like that could give a man bruises and back scratches and leave him exhausted. A hard-fought tussle can fire up a man's loins. He felt a twitch in his groan. *Damn you, Rawlings.* Now, Stryker must make a difficult decision. He wasn't exactly eager to throw his ass down that hole but staying in the mansion with Rawlings presented… complexities. He wasn't sure which was more dangerous. It was not physically dangerous with her, although *that was* a possibility. He grunted aloud at that. She *was* an unknown. It made her damn appealing. No, dangerous in the sense of having Rawlings get inside his head. Not enough room in there with Morgan. *Fuck.*

"Ah, hell!" Stryker leaped down the hole.

He kept his feet together, his arms crossed on his chest, and his eyes closed. He fell straight down the first ten feet. Then he felt shaft pressure on his back as the tunnel chute shifted away from a straight vertical drop toward a more gradual twenty-degree incline. The steel casing with tight welding joints allowed for a smooth ride. After having traveled one hundred feet in total darkness, Stryker slid at a much slower speed, having him think he might live.

An escape passage for Hopkins and his wife, which is where Stryker now figured he was. It had to end where the stop wouldn't kill a person. He thought about the clever commode handle and then began to enjoy the ride. The ride ended in another one hundred feet when his boots hit a wooden door flap and Stryker's body slid from the tube and landed in a cargo net. A modicum of light peeked at him from in front. He rolled off the webbing onto hands and knees and collected his senses before getting to his feet.

Thinking they ought to charge for that ride, he tried looking around in the dim light. He was in a small room the size of a double-hole outhouse, a little bigger, but not much. The light escaped from the edges of a door four and a half feet in height, curved at the top. Hard to tell in the faint light. He reached for it, misjudged the distance, and stumbled forward.

Another body shot from the tube and landed in the cargo net. "Whew! What a ride!" Rawlings exclaimed.

Stryker told himself he should not have been surprised. If he had thought about what she would do after he jumped into the chute, he might have guessed she would jump in after him. He wasn't thinking about her, though. He was more occupied with where he was going after he leaped into the tube. He'd made two leaps, one in, one away, away from temptation. He thought it was away. Turned out that with Rawlings in the cargo net, he hadn't leaped away after all. That's okay. He liked the girl.

"All right, Rawlings. Let's see where this comes out." He let her untangle herself from the netting while he held his hands in front and searched for the latch on the dwarf-sized door. He found it and stepped back to pull it open. Rawlings bumped into him when he stepped back.

"Oomph! Hello dear," Rawlings said cheerfully.

Stryker let it pass. He bent down and stepped through the small doorway and into a sewage tunnel made from clay bricks. Light came through an iron gate on the other side of the sewage stream. The gate opened out onto a street. Stryker saw a house on the other side of the narrow street. A wooden walkover allowed them to cross the stream without wading through sewage. There wasn't a lock on the gate. *Who would want to steal sewage?*

Stryker and Rawlings emerged from the tunnel onto Joice Street near Pine. Joice Street was a deserted back alley. The sewage tunnel emptied into the marshland near Embarcadero.

"Bodies could be picked up here in the dead of night and no one would be the wiser," Rawlings observed.

"Or farther down in marshland."

"I guess that solves the disappearing bodies. Now what, Stryker"

Stryker remembered the smell in the mansion and thought about bringing it up. Instead, he growled, "Gotta kill Jace and Jude." He turned and walked fifteen paces to Pine Street and then on up the hill to Powell.

"Naturally, of course." Rawlings fell in behind Stryker, jogging every few steps to keep up with his long strides.

They waited fifteen minutes at the corner to catch the cable car and rode it down to Market Street. It was another ten minutes to wait for the ride to the Palace Hotel.

Stryker and Rawlings never made it back to the Hopkins mansion that night. Nor did they ever find out who, or what, still roamed inside the house calling for Mary.

George Hearst, Stryker, and Rawlings exchanged information about Jace and Jude over breakfast later in the morning. During the second meeting, the senator, who sat across the table from Stryker and Rawlings, spent more time eyeing Rawlings than he did Stryker. His fascination was not with her beauty. He wanted to ask if she was Stryker's sister, but he didn't.

The grill room filled up fast. Business deals were being made. Cigar smoke, even in the early morning, created a low-hanging cloud that hovered over the tables. Rawlings was the lone woman in the men's grill room. Very few females were welcome in the grill room: women like Morgan, or in this case, another guest of Hearst. The staff did not question Stryker. For obvious reasons, he was a friend of Hearst, and Stryker's menacing countenance as well as the well-used Peacemaker he carried were deterrents. On one occasion, the grill room staff politely asked Stryker to conform to custom. That did not go well for the staff members. Hearst intervened, but only after the maître d almost had his throat cut. It was an unpleasant disturbance. After that, exceptions were allowed. It was good to have powerful friends like Senator George Hearst, and… Mister Colt.

"Turns out," Rawlings said. "Jace and Jude have an affiliation with the Working Man's Party in San Francisco, a Marxist organization headed up by a man named Denis Kearney."

Hearst knew about the Working Man's Party before Rawlings told him her inquiries had connected the family's killers to the Marxist group.

"I thought the son of a bitch was dead," Hearst said, reaching for a biscuit and using his knife to slather on some butter. "He caused a lot of trouble when building the railroads. Hated Chinese and hated Capitalism. Miserable Irish bastard. "Sorry, Miss," Hearst apologized to Rawlings.

"Sounds like the bastard is still causing problems," Rawlings countered, showing the senator there was no need for apologies.

"Need to find Jace and Jude," Stryker growled.

Hearst knew why; there was no need to ask. He wouldn't ask the woman with Stryker, either. Hearst figured that much based on how she resembled the man beside her.

"I had inquiries made about passengers leaving San Francisco from the Ferry House in the last two days," Hearst said. "On a hunch, your two men might be wanting to get out of town. A Jace Slocum and a Jude Chatlog boarded trains headed south. Two different trains, six hours apart, and both appeared to have a couple of men traveling with them. The ticket agent believes they were going to San Juan Bautista. He said he heard them talking about a meeting there. The Southern Pacific Railroad does not go to San Juan Bautista. It bypassed the mission to run south to Salinas. The six men bought tickets to Prunedale, which is about twelve miles south of the junction road to the mission. They would have to leave the train at the junction and get horses, wagon, or walk the three miles to the mission." Hearst reached for the coffee pot and refilled his cup. "That's all I got for right now."

"Thank you, Senator," Rawlings said. "You have been very helpful. I can report that to my superiors in Washington." Rawlings drew a deep breath and shook her head in apology. "Sorry, I cannot tell you who they are right now."

"I would like to know." Hearst smiled.

"Of course." Rawlings returned his smile. "Perhaps later."

Stryker cut into his breakfast steak.

"You'll be traveling to San Juan Bautista, Stryker," Hearst stated flatly. He got no answer from the mixed breed. "I suppose you don't want any help."

Again, there was no reply.

Pleasantries were exchanged between Hearst and Rawlings for the remainder of the breakfast. Stryker pushed back his plate, drained the last of his coffee, and rose from the table. He and Hearst exchanged nods. Rawlings extended her hand. Hearst shook it and that ended the second breakfast meeting.

"Two train tickets to Prunedale. I'm buying," Rawlings said to

Stryker, as they walked across the lobby where guests were waiting in long lines to check out of the hotel.

Stryker let Rawlings go ahead of him, pretending he was delayed by hotel guests getting in his way and he watched her from behind. He felt a strange connection to her, a liking, a kindred spirit with her, which was odd. Stryker never had kindred spirits with anyone, except Morgan, of course. That kindredship involved political, philosophical, and physical attraction. Rawlings had none of those attractions for him, yet he felt a peculiar kinship with her. He wondered why.

He caught up to her and took her by the arm. "This could be dangerous, Rawlings."

Outside the Palace Hotel, they caught a cable car to take them to the Ferry House. The car was crowded. Stryker and Rawlings sat scrunched together on the bench. Stryker rested his hands on his knees, rather than make more room by circling an arm around Rawlings. During the short ride to the station, Rawlings reached over and ran her fingers around on the back of his hand. She held her hand on his momentarily, squeezed it, and then let go.

What did she mean by that? Stryker looked at Rawlings. She returned his gaze with a warm smile. He felt a rush of awkwardness and faced forward.

Long lines stretched from the ticket windows, and they queued up behind the one titled "LOS ANGELES." In addition to their tickets, they bought tickets for Stryker's roan and a mare they rented from the Ferry House stable for Rawlings. Forty minutes and two mugs of coffee later, they boarded the Southern Pacific train headed south.

The coach was packed, and Stryker was not able to get his customary seat in the back. He could have if he had been by himself. He did not necessarily sense any additional vulnerability or danger from passengers seated behind him. He'd checked them out before sitting down next to Rawlings. He was just irritated he couldn't take his normal seat. Habits, Stryker had them. He was getting grumpy in his thirties. Though it was those kinds of habits that had kept him alive.

The couplings clanged up the tracks and the train jerked forward. Stryker and Rawlings settled in for the four-hour ride to the San

Bautista junction. He sat on the aisle. Rawlings sat next to him. Their seats were part of a four-seat configuration which allowed for easy conversation among four passengers. A woman sat across from them. She appeared to be in her midfifties.' Seemingly traveling alone, she looked out the window.

Beside the woman was a young man in his late twenties, or early thirties. He was a neat diminutive, little man with a neat little mustache. He had short black wavy hair, neatly parted in the middle, and a perpetual neat little smirk on his face.

He appeared to be one of those men who always knew more than anyone and made it a habit of making sure you knew it too. He was a haughty little man, an immediate dislike. Stryker would not need much provocation for him to reach across the narrow space and slap the shit out of him.

Rawlings eyed the man and woman with more curiosity than disdain, and after twenty miles with short stops in Burlingame and Redwood City, she asked, "Where are you headed?" She purposely did not address either of them directly, allowing one or both to respond. Their choice. The woman did.

"Los Angeles," she replied, turning from the window with a gracious smile. "And you two?" she asked. "I suppose you are together. I saw you in line together to buy tickets."

"San Juan Bautista," Rawlings said.

Stryker was mildly irritated when Rawlings supplied that information. Though he couldn't say why it bothered him. Stryker stared at the little man as if daring the fellow to piss him off. *Forget manners.*

"Oh, that is such a charming place," the woman gushed. "The mission there has three-day music festivals for people to enjoy, and art fairs, too." She broadened her smile. "My name is Audrey, Audrey Caswell." Audrey dipped her head to her right. "His name is Nick. It took me half an hour to get that out of him. He has a thick accent from somewhere in Eastern Europe, I guess. Does not like to talk."

"I'm Rawlings. He's Stryker." Rawlings returned the friendly smile. "You have interest in Los Angeles?"

"I have a sister who is not well."

"Sorry to hear that. I hope your company will bring better health for your sister." Rawlings smile morphed into a show of concern. She addressed the man. "Are you also going to Los Angeles?"

Stryker resisted the urge to elbow Rawlings's ribs.

"In fact, I am," he answered with a fractured smile. Maybe it hurt.

"Well, I hope you have a pleasant journey." Rawlings broke off the conversation after that. She wasn't inclined to learn more about an ill sister, and she gave up on Nick. She could tell drawing words out of him was like pulling his teeth and just as painful. She closed her eyes and leaned her head against Stryker's shoulder.

Stryker stretched out his legs under Nick's bench and tipped the Stetson down over his brow.

You may not have heard of Nick. You might know something about his work, though. Nikola is his correct first name. Traveling out West, he sought to satisfy his intense curiosity. He wanted to see the real West. A Serbian American engineer and inventor, he worked in laboratories he had set up in New York and Colorado Springs. Incidentally, his last name was Tesla. He was an extremely bright fellow, a resolute bachelor all his life; he could do integral calculus in his head. Other than a modern mode of transportation named after him, he invented the use of electricity with alternating current. Held three hundred patents in electricity, wireless communications, and power generation. He worked at Edison Machine Works in New York but only met Thomas Edison a couple of times. He quit there over a pay dispute. Edison's direct electrical current did provide lightbulb illumination, but it was more dangerous because its power interruption was more difficult. Alternating electrical current is far more effective for household purposes and is in use all over the world. It is used to light up your house today… or at night. Despite all the patents, Tesla was never able to become permanently, financially independent. He died in his New York City hotel room, bankrupt, at the age of eighty-six, leaving behind a five-figure unpaid hotel bill–and a flock of pigeons he called friends. He did try to pay his hotel bill with a patent on a death ray.

Stryker and Rawlings left the train at the San Juan Bautista junction and never saw Nikola or Audrey again. Rawlings briefly wondered if Nikola and Audrey spoke during the remainder of their trip. Stryker busied himself unloading the horses.

The road to the mission wound through rolling grass-covered hills. A few trees dotted the landscape. A eucalyptus grove and a stubby California buckeye tree here and there were the indigenous species. The land flattened out as the mission came into sight.

Stryker reined the roan to a halt and Rawlings drew up beside him. He dismounted and pulled a set of binoculars from the saddlebag. Rawlings stepped from the mare and followed him to a small knoll where Stryker stretched out in a prone position to use the field glasses. Stryker preferred to lie down so he could steady the glasses with his elbows firmly planted on the ground. A habit he learned in the Army when adjusting artillery fire. He also lay down back then to present a smaller target for snipers.

Rawlings, thinking Stryker wanted to reduce his silhouette for whatever reason, lay on the ground next to him, but she had not called in artillery fire. "See anything?"

The mission rested on flat ground three-quarters of a mile away from where they lay. Stryker talked as he looked through the field glasses, "The mission building, a cross on the roof, and a line of separate rooms run off to the left. Crowd in front of the main building. Twenty or thirty. Shit."

"Could be the music festival Audrey spoke about," Rawlings whispered.

Stryker ignored why Rawlings whispered and replied in a normal voice. "Yeah, maybe." He lowered the glasses and propped himself up on an elbow. "Gonna need your help."

"What do you need me to do?"

"Could be giving out room assignments." Stryker surmised if the priest were giving a talk, the crowd would be either sitting inside the main building or seated somewhere else more comfortable. Anyway, his guess was not far off. "If those people are going to be staying in rooms tonight, I want to know where Jace and Jude's rooms are."

"I see." Rawlings did not follow up by asking why Stryker wanted to know that. "And you want me to find out."

"Ride in, join in like you've come for the festival."

"So, if I see Jace and Jude, find out where the two are staying, how do I get that to you?" Rawlings asked eagerly, sounding all in with the plan.

"I'll ride in about midnight." Stryker handed the binoculars to Rawlings. "I'll meet you outside at the corner of the last room."

"Midnight," Rawlings repeated. "But I don't have a—"

"Me neither. Sundown's around eight. Figure four hours after that." Stryker realized he was asking a lot of Rawlings. He thought she could manage it. She acted like it, anyway, and she had shown how she could do things on her own at the Hopkin's mansion. He also counted on Jace and Jude not getting a good look at Rawlings during the shooting. They may not have even known there was a woman with him. They were calculated assumptions.

Without another word, Rawlings got to her feet and strode fifty paces to the mare. She was all business. She put her foot in the stirrup and swung into the saddle. She gave Stryker a nod as she rode past.

Stryker watched Rawlings ride across the flat terrain until she got to the mission. He hoped she kept the .38 within easy reach and out of sight, if necessary, but within easy reach. He felt a twang of guilt, asking her to do something that could be dangerous.

He led the roan to an elderberry bush, tied off the reins, and poured water into his hat for the horse to drink. Normally he used a halter to secure the animal, but this day he might need to move quickly. He took the field glasses with him and went back to the grassy knoll. By this time, he couldn't see Rawlings or the mare, nor could he see her in the crowd. The crowd now looked smaller. Some of the group had already gone to their rooms, he guessed. He lowered the glasses and rested his chin on his forearm.

Rawlings? Who is this woman? There was something about her. She was similar but different from Morgan. *Morgan?* What did he know about her before meeting in Egalitaria? Nothing.

If Stryker were to find out more about Morgan's past, he might learn she was a precocious child with one sibling, a brother who was three years older than her. She grew up playing games with him and his two friends. They did not play regular games like hide and go seek, red rover come over, or spin the bottle. Besides, how are you going to play that with three boys and one girl? No, the four of them made up mental exercise games, using math puzzles, sequential discovery puzzles, or historical questions. Sometimes the boys would make wooden or metal puzzles for assembly. Their games were inventive and complex, and Morgan always did well with them. She did not often win, nevertheless, she produced intelligent, reasonable alternatives that the four of them debated with considerable thoughtful exchange.

When Morgan reached her early teens, her parents sent her to the New England Academy for Gifted Children in Boston, where her brother was already attending. Morgan's brother excelled in science and biology, whereas Morgan took a liking to science and math. Her brother eventually became a surgeon. Morgan gravitated toward engineering, uncommon for a female. Upon graduating from the academy, she was offered scholarships to the Massachusetts Institute of Technology and a fledging university in faraway Golden, Colorado, called Colorado School of Mines. Morgan said her goodbyes, packed her study materials along with her clothing, and boarded the train to Colorado.

She excelled at the university, majoring in Geological Engineering, being the only female in her class. She earned respect from the professors and resentment from her male peers. One of the male students defended her against the males, a young man named Nathanial Bickford, who was also studying Geological Engineering. Their friendship grew, and during their senior year, they bonded in marriage. The two bright mining engineers struck out on their own after graduation and built an empire in gold mining and ranching. That empire was taken from them by a gang of Marxist politicos who came to their town named Bickford and changed its name to Egalitaria. In the process, the gang murdered Nathanial. Morgan, now widowed with a teenage son, lost the mines and ranch to Egalitaria's new collective. Morgan, alone and desperate to gain back her property, turned to a stranger who had ridden into town to retrieve his stolen horse. An unlikely savior, the stranger was a vicious killer and wanted for murder, a murder he did commit. But he was proficient with gun and blade, the kind of man she needed. That man lay on a grassy knoll, looking out at the town of San Juan Bautista.

It was doubtful Stryker would ask Morgan to relate any of her past or her childhood to him. The fact that he had yet to do so already suggested he would not make such inquiries. One reason for the mixed breed's reticence was that asking Morgan about her history might serve as an invitation to ask about his.

Hours dragged on. Stryker made numerous trips to the roan. He led it to water at a small creek and to feed on ryegrass that grew near the stream. Each time he returned to the grassy lookout, he raised the field glasses to search around the mission and look for Rawlings. He was not able to see her again. When dusk arrived and it was too dark to effectively see anything that distant, he put the binoculars in the saddlebag. At approximately two and a half hours after sundown, Stryker mounted the roan and while holding it a slow walk, angled his way to within a quarter mile of the mission. He remembered seeing a stand of juniper trees in the binoculars about two hundred paces off the road and reined the roan away from the trail to look for it. It took a while in the dim light but eventually, the dark shapes of the trees appeared. He tied the roan to one of the rugged little trees and waited another hour or so, using the field glasses every few minutes.

Behind him he heard a wagon drive up the road; there were people on it, young men, and women, shouting, laughing, and having a fun time. Stryker figured they were on their way to the festival. Unable to see them or the wagon, he only heard the commotion. Then he was able to make out a hay wagon with a group of ten or more young people riding on it. Two horses pulled the wagon. Stryker watched them drive on up to the mission and jump off in front of the main building. They entered the mission's front door, leaving one person to drive the wagon around the back of the building.

Stryker got anxious about Rawlings. Closer to the mission, he tried again to find her using the field glasses, but it was no good. Was she able to find and use a clock in the mission? *Damn, should not have let her come with me.* He did not have a good feeling about things.

The moon overhead was little more than a fingernail. There was not much lunar light off that. Even with ambient light from lanterns that hung outside the mission, it was too dark to see where the twenty rooms, or so, ended. It was too shadowed. It looked like twenty rooms. Could have been more. Could have been less.

Stryker estimated he spent another hour and a half waiting before he pulled the Winchester from the saddle boot and started on foot toward the mission. Using the North Star's position as a time reference, as he did during night-time artillery exercises, he figured it must be getting close to midnight. He walked back on the road and stayed on it until he was within two hundred yards of the mission. None of the visitors remained out front. He thought they must be in the chapel, gathered in the courtyard out back, or in their rooms. He hoped they were in their rooms.

The road ended in front of the main building of the mission. The missionaries learned to use mud tiles on their roofs because Native Americans shot flaming arrows on thatched roofs. Stryker got off the road and crept toward the rooms. As he got closer, he realized the openings he had seen with the field glasses were not doorways. They were arched spaces between adobe brick pillars. A tiled walkway ran behind the openings and the room's doors were on the far side of the walkway. A large oak tree grew at the left end with a wooden bench beneath its branches. A person sat on the bench.

Rawlings. It had to be. *Good.* Stryker quickened his pace.

"Stryker." Rawlings spoke in a whisper.

Stryker looked around before he sat with her. They were alone except for the mare tied to the tree. He kept the carbine lying across his thighs with a hand on the trigger guard. "You see 'em?" Stryker asked, meaning Jace and Jude.

"Yes," Rawlings replied with what seemed to Stryker was a labored whisper.

"Any trouble?"

"I asked too many questions. They got suspicious." She spoke with effort.

"Rawlings?" Stryker could tell something was wrong.

"Room thirteen."

"Jace and Jude."

Rawlings nodded.

"You hurt?"

"They cut my stomach." Suddenly Rawlings inhaled sharply and bent over groaning. "Left me in room twelve," she rasped. "Ohhh… God dammit."

"You need a doctor." Stryker slid his arm under her legs, the other around her waist, and started to lift. The carbine clattered to the ground.

"No. Stop, it's too late." Rawlings leaned back against Stryker's arm. "Kiss me."

"Rawlings!"

"Kiss me."

"Then we go." Stryker leaned down and brushed his lips on hers.

Rawlings took another deep breath. She gathered her strength and raised her face to Stryker. "We're half brother and sister."

Stryker lifted her from the bench, ignoring what Rawlings just said.

"We have the same father. I'm a 'Stryker' too." Rawlings dropped her chin.

"C'mon." But her body had gone limp. He lowered her back on the bench. "Rawlings?" He felt her neck for a pulse. "Rawlings," he whispered.

Rawlings was dead. Stryker stood and stared down at her body. She had slumped sideways onto the bench. The pistol was missing. They must have wrestled it away from her before she could use it. "Dammit." *Rawlings, Stryker, what was your first name? I'll never know it.* He knew what she told him was true. It all made sense now. Her facial features, the puzzling inner connection. "Ah, shit, Rawlings."

A faint light reflection on the Winchester's barrel caught Stryker's eye. He picked up the gun. Held it for a moment, his left hand was around the front stock, the other in the looped lever. He worked the lever, seated the.44 round, and took off for room *thirteen*.

The bloody handprints along the wall ignited Stryker's anger.

The door to room *thirteen* was closed but unlocked. Stryker turned the doorknob and pushed open the door. He stepped inside the twelve-by-twelve room. Taking his left hand off the gun, he locked the door.

Jace and Jude sat at a table in the center of the room. Two other men also sat at the table. Two were standing. All six froze, staring at the man who had just entered their room with a rifle.

Jace took the first bullet in his chest, Jude the second at the base of his throat. The two men at the table jumped to their feet. The standing men leaped over the bed to escape the bullets.

There were no windows and only one door. Stryker stood at the door and pumped the lever after each round fired. Firing rapidly, he put a.44 round in each man who was with Jace and Jude. Stryker walked past them on the floor and shot the two men who were cowering behind the bed. It was all over in less than five seconds. He killed six.

Stryker left the room, walking past the bloody handprints to the bench where her body rested. He took a final look at Rawlings and untied the mare.

He led the mare onto the road and strode into the night. Stryker heard shouting coming from the mission. A woman who had run into Rawlings coming out of room *twelve* had gone for help and returned with several others. The woman would later tell the sheriff that the injured woman told her the men in room *thirteen* had knifed her.

Stryker booted the Winchester, untied the roan, and came around to its side. He stretched his arms to the saddle, but he hesitated and leaned against the leather rigging. *She came out to meet me instead of getting medical help.* Stryker slumped his head against the saddle. "Dammit, God!" He stood there until the roan nickered a half-minute later. Then he put a boot in the stirrup and swung onto the saddle. Holding the mare's reins, Stryker guided the roan onto the road leading back to the rail junction.

Some could say the mixed breed was a callous man with no regard for the dead. That was true. Stryker was a pragmatist. When his wife was killed many years ago, he left her body lying on the bloody ground and rode away. To him, the dead no longer exist. They are gone, never to be again. So, when he rode away, leaving Rawlings' body on the bench, he was not leaving her. She had already left him.

As for his comment to the deity, that was not a disrespectful curse. Stryker was not an atheist; neither was he a religious man. He and God just left each other alone. Stryker was merely expressing grief. One could call his outburst prayerful anguish if they wished and leave it at that.

A stiff breeze made the night seem colder. Stryker buttoned his collar. Three miles to the junction dragged on, the roan and mare had nothing to say, and Stryker was alone with his thoughts. Rawlings occupied most of them. *Why didn't she tell him sooner? But even if she had, what would their relationship have been?* Stryker was not a family man. He would not attend family gatherings, or chat with relatives, or her relatives. But then again, Rawlings didn't seem the type either. *Where did she get the name Rawlings? Had she been married? Was she married now? Was there a husband to be notified?*

She would be alive now if he had not sent her ahead to the mission. The realization hit him suddenly. She would be riding on the mare next to him. Stryker glanced back at the mare's empty saddle.

"Fuck it. I don't know when the train stops, or if it will stop at the junction." Stryker spoke aloud, pulling himself away from Rawlings. There was no station at the junction, no train schedule posted, only a wood-planked platform and livestock ramp. He could wait for the train or ride the rail's maintenance road to Gilroy. Stryker reined the roan onto the maintenance road. Better to do that than sit around, waiting for the train. He should have checked to find out when the train next stopped at the junction before getting off the train. *Rawlings*. It would take some time to get her out of his head. *Damn, Rawlings.*

Gilroy lay fourteen miles north with a few communities where the train did not stop. The land was flat; it was an easy ride. It would be getting light when he got to Gilroy. If he had an hour's wait or more for the train, he could feed and water the horses and get breakfast too. These things he could do. He could busy himself. In the meantime, he had a five-hour ride to Gilroy, and Rawlings would ride along with him. Which she did, in his head… and in his chest.

A train traveling north past Stryker and that was about halfway to Gilroy. That gave him a bit of satisfaction since he would have waited two and half hours sitting at the junction for it. He would rather be on the trail even if it meant a longer trip to town. The roan and mare offered no complaints.

The sun was up for a good half-hour when Stryker rode into Gilroy. It had been a long night, a long night of heavy gnawing in his chest. Nothing he could do to stop it. No bullet nor blade to kill it.

It was good to see the sun come up. A new day. Stryker watered the roan and mare at the first horse trough he came to in town. He got feed for them at *Jacob's Livery* and sponged the horses down while they ate. He stabled them and walked to the train station to check on the train times. The next train was at 9:35. He had a couple of hours.

"Edith's Eats," read the sign hanging in front of a restaurant across from the station, and it looked open. It smelled open as well. The aroma of sausage and bacon wafted its way to Stryker. He could use a hot cup of strong black coffee too. He crossed the street to Edith's.

Inside, there were thirteen tables aligned in four rows, three in each row, except one table by window with two chairs. Each table was covered with navy-blue tablecloths. The kitchen sat in the rear, accessed by a swinging half-door and fronted by a waist-high counter supporting the cash register and two glass racks of pastries. The restaurant was crowded with many tables already taken. The table by the window was empty, and Stryker took it. A young man, appearing to be in his midteens rushed to Stryker's table for his food order. His name badge read, "Jimmy."

Fresh-faced with light brown wavy hair and wearing a navy-blue apron, the waiter asked Stryker, "What would you like, sir?"

I'd like you to bring Rawlings back to life. Stryker wanted to say. Instead, he said, "Eggs over easy, slice of ham, and black coffee."

"Thank you, sir." Jimmy wrote the order on a paper pad, spun sharply, and marched off.

Stryker watched out the window. A train pulled into the station, arriving from the north. The black engine puffed steam. A tender car hauled coal, two coach cars, a baggage car, a cattle car, and a caboose. *Baggage car–can it hold all my regrets?*

"Your coffee, sir." Jimmy placed a mug of steaming black coffee in front of Stryker. He hadn't seen the waiter approach; he was still peering out the window judging the size of the baggage car.

Stryker turned to his coffee, pleased to see the brew hot and black and in a mug. He lifted the mug and inhaled the aroma before sipping. *Edith makes a good cup*, he thought. He set the cup on the table, keeping his hands around the mug. Gazing into the coffee, Stryker's mind lingered on the baggage car. *Regrets. I got a trainload of 'em, all right. I won't have nightmares about Rawlings, though. Those are reserved for Leigh. Still, my fuck-up cost Rawlings her life.* Stryker blew a heavy breath into the mug, briefly dissipating the small rising wisp of vapor. Stryker was not a perfect man. Not even close. He did not strive to be. However, if he cut himself a little slack, he might consider the last perfect man got nailed to a cross for his virtue.

The eggs and ham were good too. *Good on Edith.* Stryker ate slowly. He had time. After the second cup of the strong brew, he paid for breakfast and left Edith's to collect the horses.

The train was on time. Stryker read a copy of the *San Francisco Examiner* while he waited in the station.

CHAPTER TEN

Stryker stepped on the coach with eight other passengers and was able to secure his preferred seat in the rear, facing forward. Another man and woman already sat across from Stryker's bench, facing rearward. Why someone would prefer to face rearward when a forward seat was available did not cross Stryker's mind. He took his seat and scooted next to the window. No one sat next to him.

The conversation between the man and woman was terse whispering. Stryker maintained his gaze out the window but could not help overhearing the arguing. The man, a young man in his early twenties was not a strikingly handsome fellow. The woman, or girl—she seemed a year or two younger than her debate partner—would not be considered a prized catch either. The issue concerned a perceived betrayal by the young man. Whether there was such a perfidy, Stryker could not tell. The fellow denied it as much as he could without raising his voice.

Finally, when they noticed Stryker's fixated stare on them, the young adults broke off the argument. "Our apologies, sir," the male ruefully began. "We were just having a friendly squabble. Sorry to disturb you."

Stryker returned to gazing out the window. He wanted no part in their discussion, nor did he want a conversation.

"Are you traveling to San Francisco?" the girl asked in a delightfully sweet voice. "We are going there too," she added, not waiting for Stryker's response. A response that never came.

"We're sorry if we bothered you." The girl reached out her hand to touch Stryker's knee. "Are you upset about something? You look kind of sad."

Stryker's faraway gaze out the window must have betrayed him. The menacing stare he gave them portrayed no sorrow. Nonetheless, the girl's perception caught him by surprise. Before Stryker could think of a better response, like ignoring her, he said, "No."

"We came out to California to see what it is like. We've heard so much about it."

Stryker turned to what was on the other side of the glass.

"Please don't be mad at us," the girl pleaded. She had one of those faces which was round and flat, and plain, which made her eyes look bigger. She took advantage of her eyes by holding them widely open when she talked.

Stryker turned away from the window. *Now what?* He looked first at the young woman, and then at the man beside her, before replying, "No problem."

"I'm Cathy." Cathy placed a hand on her friend's arm. "He's Frank." Cathy then raised her eyebrows to Stryker as if asking for his name.

"Stryker."

Cathy stretched out her hand. "Glad to meet you, Mister Stryker."

Many things flashed through Stryker's mind. None were friendly. However, he chose to make use of the diversion the couple presented and shook her hand.

"Frank is a draftsman. He is in between jobs. Starts work next month in Chicago. He wanted to see the West. We really liked Arizona. It's like the real West." Cathy was rolling, chatty.

"Draftsman." Stryker was trying.

"Yes, I'll work for Adler and Sullivan in Chicago," Frank added.

"It's one of the largest design firms in Chicago. They had a big fire there in 1871. Burned the town down. Huge conflagration. It took years to rebuild," he supplied.

"Heard about the fire."

"What line of work do you do, Mister Stryker?" Cathy wanted to know.

"Odd jobs."

"Like a handyman." Cathy nodded knowingly.

"Yes."

Frank and Cathy did not pursue what type of handy work Stryker performed, perhaps after noticing the.44 Peacemaker and correctly assuming it was his tool of trade.

Stryker had about all he could stand. He let them know the discussion was over by leaning back and pulling the Stetson down over his brow.

Frank and Catherine did marry the following year, although it ended in divorce in 1922. Frank married again in 1923. That also ended in divorce, four years later. He had taken up with a woman named Mamah in 1909, whom he did not marry. A beautiful lass, but she was brutally murdered along with six others by a staff member while Frank was away. The murderous staff member later committed suicide over what he had done. Finally, Frank married a woman named Olgivanna, who was from Montenegro. They married in 1928 and remained married until 1959, the year Frank died. "Olgi" died in 1985.

Frank Lloyd Wright had gone on to become one of the premier architects of all time. He eschewed the historical European designs of French, Italian, and other designs of old architecture, and built structures with straight lines, and sharp angles. Form followed function in his work. Many claim the book, *The Fountainhead*, by Ayn Rand, is loosely based on his life.

Stryker kept the hat over his brow until he heard the conductor announce the train arriving in San Francisco. He used a forefinger to tip the brim of his hat up. Frank and Cathy noticed his supposed awakening and said nothing. Cathy offered Stryker a friendly smile. That was all. The train conductor continued with additional announcements about other train connections and times. Frank and Cathy busied themselves, looking out the window. The train locomotive rolled inside the Ferry House made such a racket reverberating off the walls, that it would have been difficult to talk, anyway. *Good.*

Once he stepped from the train, Stryker had the horses unloaded from the livestock car and returned the rented mare to the Ferry House stable. The stableboy led it to the back of the stable and that reminder of Rawlings disappeared into a stall. There would be more reminders of his half sister over the next day or two. He arranged for the roan to get watered, fed, curried, and wiped down before he walked out of the stable.

It was just past eleven o'clock when Stryker entered the Palace Hotel. He strode through the front entrance and went straight to the reception desk.

"The senator was still having late breakfast in the men's grill if you want to see him," the hotel attaché informed Stryker. "He has a young lady with him." Stryker figured the attaché added that information so the decision on whether to interrupt Hearst was up to him.

Stryker was not in a courteous mood. He abruptly left the reception desk and marched to the men's grill room. He saw Hearst in his regular booth along the left wall. The senator sat with his back to Stryker. The girl across the table from Hearst noticed Stryker when he entered the room. Her shoulder-length auburn hair was not flaming red; it had a darker tint, and she had freckles. She was slight of build and pretty. Not Stryker's preference, but nevertheless, the girl was nice looking. She eyed Stryker through round tortoise glasses. She wore a white blouse with an upturned collar, looking collegial. She continued to watch him as he made his way to Hearst's table.

Stryker took a seat beside the girl to face Hearst. She quickly scooted away. You could tell she was not pleased he joined Hearst and her at the table, but she did not say anything. She just looked annoyed.

"Hello there, Stryker," Hearst greeted, hiding his surprise well.

"George."

"Stryker, I'd like you to meet Miss Bosworth, Kate Bosworth."

Miss Kate Bosworth, still recovering from the mixed breed's sudden appearance, did not offer her hand when Stryker dipped the Stetson.

"I was just telling her about you, that you might accompany her to the Hopkins mansion," Hearst said, then he added, "I got a copy of a police telegram about an hour ago." The senator cleared his throat. "Excuse me, Kate, while I talk with him for a minute."

"Would you like me to leave?" Kate asked, politely.

"Oh no, you can listen," Hearst said to Kate with a kind, fatherly grin. "Apparently, they had a massacre at the Bautista Mission, six men in a room and a woman outside." The senator's face turned dark. He straightened and looked around the grill. "Oh no, Rawlings. Don't tell me…"

"She's dead." Stryker said, flatly.

Kate Bosworth jerked around at Stryker.

"Well…" Hearst glanced at Kate, inhaled, and released a long breath. Then turning to Stryker he said, "Maybe you can tell me more about that later."

"Would you like to order, sir?" The young waiter had appeared at the table without being noticed.

Hearst glanced at Kate." You ready to order, young lady?" She nodded.

"Ma'am?" The waiter addressed Miss Bosworth first.

"French toast for me and a bowl of fruit. Orange juice to drink."

"French toast sounds good to me, too," Hearst said. "Make it ham instead of fruit, and black coffee."

"Sir, your usual?" the young waiter asked Stryker, with his pencil poised over the paper pad.

Stryker always had steak and eggs at the Palace, with eggs over easy, toast, and coffee, black and strong. "Bring the coffee in a mug." That was a first for Stryker. He had put up with his brew in the hotel's dainty little flowered porcelain cups, which he immensely disliked for too long. The cups were awkward to hold and besides, they blemished his manhood. Today, after much time and patience, he'd had enough. He should have gotten coffee in a mug sooner.

"Sir, I'm… not sure… we have—" the waiter began.

Stryker cut him off. "Then find something else."

The waiter spun sharply and walked away.

"Now, where were we?" Hearst asked. "Ah yes, I think I was about to suggest Stryker accompany you to the Hopkins house when you go there, Kate."

A horrified look sprang on Kate's face. Her eyes flashed large and white.

Hearst had to laugh. "Kate, I can think of no one else you'd be safer with." The senator chuckled.

Stryker turned from Hearst to Kate. "Get her someone else." He was not eager to go back to the mansion. Didn't need more reminders.

"No, Stryker. You go." Hearst knew Stryker would honor his request if asked firmly. Hearst and Stryker had a tacit agreement about the tasks the senator gave Stryker. Hearst paid him. Stryker performed them. Hearst asked no questions. Even though Hearst had mentioned a later discussion about the massacre, he would not bring it up again. He knew what happened at the mission. Stryker killed the men. The Rawlings woman was killed in the process.

"I'll do it."

Kate attempted to regain her composure. "Well, sir, if you feel… but wouldn't a policeman, or, I don't know, a security guard?" Kate scrunched her face. "I can just go by myself. I'm not afraid." She had a tiny quiver in her voice.

Hearst and Stryker noticed it. The two men exchanged glances. "It's settled," Hearst said. "I suggest you go right after our breakfast. I will arrange for a hotel carriage to take both of you to the mansion." The senator focused his attention on Miss Bosworth while he spoke. Then, turning to Stryker he said, "Stryker, Morgan will be arriving back in town sometime this afternoon. Thought you might like to know," Hearst said.

Stryker nodded.

The waiter brought food and coffee at the same time. Hearst and Kate got their French toast, fruit and ham, coffee, and juice. Stryker got his steak and eggs, and coffee served in a beer mug.

They ate breakfast with only a mild conversation between Hearst and Kate, asking her about college and her responding. Stryker listened while eating and cutting his steak. When finished eating and downed a couple of last sips, Stryker slid from the table, rose to his feet, and said, "Let's go, Kate."

"Uh, I need to freshen up, first." Kate slid across the seat to leave the table.

Stryker knew that was girl talk, which meant she had to use the bathroom.

"Good, while you're doing that, I'll go make arrangements for the carriage," Hearst said. He waited for Miss Bosworth to get out of earshot. "Don't let anything happen to that girl, Stryker."

Stryker acknowledged the senator's request with another nod.

Stryker and Miss Bosworth arrived at the top of Nob Hill forty-five minutes later and stepped from the cable car. They had taken Hearst's arranged carriage to the corner of Market and Powell Streets and caught the Powell Street cable car up the hill to the mansion. They walked up the long stone-paved driveway together. Stryker stole side glances at the girl. She was rail thin, wearing an ankle-length dark-blue skirt under the high-collared blouse and the sweater she had added before leaving the Palace Hotel. The top of her skirt showed off a narrow waist. Miss Bosworth strode up the inclined driveway with purpose. Stryker judged she would mature with achievement. It was just a quick assessment.

The senator also gave Kate a key to the front door. She handed it to Stryker and stood back as he used it to unlock and open the massive front door. Stryker entered ahead of Kate. Then together they walked through the dark wood-stained oak-paneled walls of the vestibule. They came to the reception room with its ornate oak and mahogany woodwork, wall paintings of people and places, the massive stone fireplace, and the unopened wall safe still lying in the middle of the floor where it had been dropped. The bodies were gone. Their blackened blood spots blended in with the dark-stained hardwood floor.

Miss Bosworth knelt next to the safe. It lay on its back with the combination lock and door facing up. It took only a moment for her to work through the numbers and open the safe. Stryker watched Kate between his glances around the room. *How did she have the combination?* It was not his business to ask.

It was a bright sunny day outside, unusual for the city of course, and Kate sifted through the paperwork she'd pulled from the safe. Stryker figured she was deciding what was important to her and what wasn't.

Stryker eyed the stairwell. The thought of when Rawlings had stood behind him on it flashed through his mind, but it was starting to fade a bit. He realized it now. Not good or bad. It was just that he knew it was happening. Morgan's impending arrival played a part. The other part was that Rawlings was taking her place behind Leigh, way behind Leigh… and Morgan… way behind Morgan, too. Still, it was too bad for Rawlings, she was the closest thing to a blood relative for Stryker, even though she was only a half-relative.

From that time on, Stryker remembered he once had a half sister. A dead half sister, and that he was partly responsible for her death.

"Maaary!" The call sounded as if it came from a male, and it came from upstairs.

"Stryker, did you hear that?" Kate leaped to her feet. She stepped closer to Stryker.

"Yeah, I heard it." *Shit.* "Stay here."

"No, I'll come with you." Kate Bosworth got converted.

They heard it again as they climbed the first set of stairs. The call came a third time when they searched the third-floor rooms.

"I'm not staying in this fucking house," Miss Bosworth declared. She gripped Stryker's arm.

Stryker grinned inwardly. *Proprieties be damned,* he mused to himself.

With Stryker's Peacemaker drawn, the two of them searched every part of the house, including all the rooms, stairwells, secret passageways, basement, and even the rooftop. They found nothing. Stryker did not believe in ghosts or the metaphysical, nevertheless, he could not explain the calls for Mary. Mary was Mark Hopkins's wife; that much Stryker knew. She left the mansion to live with another man back East. Stryker knew that too. *Could it be Mark was calling for his wife?* Stryker thought. There had to be another explanation, he reasoned. The wind or a prankster familiar with the house, he told himself.

"Let's find a case or a bag for those documents, Kate, and return to the hotel."

Kate did not argue. They found a briefcase in the office and left the Hopkins mansion that afternoon. Neither Stryker nor Miss Bosworth ever returned. Mary Hopkins never returned as well. Maybe she had heard someone calling her name and got the hell out of there. The place burned down during the 1906 earthquake, and perhaps the ghost perished in the fire.

No words were exchanged between Kate and Stryker until they got back to the Palace. In the lobby, Miss Bosworth extended her hand and said, "Thank you." Then she disappeared in a group of guests crowding toward the elevator.

Stryker tried to find Morgan.

He found her in the women's grill room. As with the men's grill, the opposite sex was not allowed. Stryker elected not to cause a scene and got a waiter to let Morgan know he was waiting for her in the hotel library.

Morgan emerged from the grill a minute later to find Stryker. They kept their distance with their greetings. That is how they were. There was no rushing into each other's arms. They were not like that.

"I need to clean up," Stryker said.

"I'll finish my meal," returned Morgan.

Stryker thought she looked damn good. She always looked attractive to him. Even when not in the best of situations. In her early thirties, five feet seven, she had straight dark-brown hair to her shoulders, hazel eyes, and high cheekbones. She stood militarily erect and was rail thin. She wore a white blouse with an upturned collar above a tan-colored leather-belted skirt.

The most admirable quality about the woman was her character, her sense of life, principles, and the values by which she lived. Morgan held that man should live his life according to his own purpose and his own objectives, free from encumbrances from others who would seek to impose their moral judgments on how to live a life. Individual freedom, freedoms guaranteed by the United States Constitution, which was the foundational cornerstone of her beliefs. Objective, not subjective, morality based on reason, and not some conjured-up dictum a morally bankrupt politician imposed on others, such as labeling a person selfish if he wanted to keep what he produced. Hers was a rational philosophy whereas the rights of the individual were to be held sacred.

Morgan Bickford had firsthand experience with such corrupt morality when she and her husband had all they had built together taken from them. Mindless townspeople supported and clamored that their wealth should be shared, in other words, stolen. In the process, they murdered her husband. EGALITARIA, that is what they renamed the town. The gang proclaimed the town citizens helped create the Bickford wealth by working for them, therefore they should share in it. Never mind the fact that the townspeople did not have the mental creativity to build the ranch and mine, nor did they borrow the money from the bank and have personal liabilities along with it. That Nathaniel and Morgan paid the workers a fair wage didn't matter.

Yes, the woman who stood before Stryker was enormously attractive. He felt it was his good fortune to have met her, and that she *chose* to be with him. "Room *eight twelve*," Stryker said.

"I just started eating my dinner," Morgan told him. "Take your time with your bath."

They were hardly words of endearment between two romantically involved people who had not seen each other in a while, but it worked for the two of them.

Morgan and Stryker walked away from each other. No hugs, no see you later.

Stryker headed to the rising room. He and four other guests loaded onto it, a couple who appeared to be a man and wife, and two elderly women. Stryker couldn't tell if the two old women were together. They stayed apart from one another. The four other guests eyed Stryker suspiciously and did not speak. The two women did get off the elevator together on the third floor. The man and woman exited on the sixth floor.

"Eighth floor, sir," the elevator operator called.

Stryker's room was located on the same floor as the senator's, but the Hearst suite was at the end of the hallway, and it occupied two rooms. Stryker inserted the key to his room and unlocked the door.

Stryker started the bath water, poured in soap, and then took off his clothing. He checked behind the bathroom door to ensure two white terrycloth robes hung there, one large, one small.

He got into the tub when it was two-thirds full and settled back in the hot soapy water, wishing soap could wash away remorse.

Morgan will be here soon. With that, Stryker washed himself. He completed his cleansing and relaxed in the hot water a few more minutes before lifting from the bathtub. He grabbed the towel and dried himself. He had just put on the larger robe, which only came down to mid-thigh, when he heard a soft knock on the door. *She must have eaten fast.*

Stryker opened the door. "Hello, Stryker."

Morgan entered and stepped closer. "I missed you," she whispered. She pulled away to look Stryker in his face. "Put your hands on me."

Stryker put his hands on both sides of Morgan's face and kissed her. Then he grasped her shoulders, spun her around, and massaged her neck and shoulders.

"That's not what I had in mind, but you have exactly one hour to stop," Morgan laughed.

"C'mon, back up with me to the chair and I'll massage you. You feel tight." Stryker guided her to the wingback where he sat in the chair and had Morgan sit on the carpet in front of him. He worked his fingers on the muscles and ligaments of her neck and her upper back, using his thumbs to make firm circling motions around her shoulder blades.

"Two hours." Morgan softly crooned. She drooped her head forward.

"Take off your blouse."

Stryker paused the rubdown while Morgan slipped off the blouse.

He hesitated to admire the bony shoulders and delicate shoulder blades, and when he touched her skin, it reminded him how smooth it was.

Stryker did not massage Morgan for two hours, but he did do the better part of an hour, massaging Morgan's neck, her shoulders, and upper and lower back. "Go relax in the tub. I'll wash you."

Stryker followed her into the bathroom where she finished undressing, and then he helped her into the clawfoot tub. Yes, it was the same water Stryker used. It remained warm, had lots of suds, and still looked clean.

He took a clean washcloth from the rack and soaped it. "Lie back and close your eyes."

Morgan dutifully did as she was told, closing her eyes, and lying back in the bathtub so that the water rose to her armpits, leaving much of her upper torso above water. Her nipples poked through the bubbles.

Stryker knelt next to the bathtub and leaned over the rim to reach Morgan. He used the washcloth and softly applied it to her face, being careful not to get soap in her eyes. He lifted her hair and washed the back of her neck, then her shoulders, and on down to her breasts. Morgan opened her eyes, and Stryker chided her to keep them closed. He then swiped the cloth around the firm mounds and paid special attention to her nipples, using the washcloth to gently pinch each little nub with a twisting motion to ensure they were properly cleansed. He lifted one of her lithe arms from the water, ran the cloth up and down, and then on each finger. He washed the other arm the same. Next, he washed her belly under the water, feeling Morgan tightening her stomach muscles as he rubbed her with the washcloth. He did both sides, having to lean farther to reach her ribs away from him.

"Keep your eyes closed," Stryker told her again as he put his free hand under her left leg and lifted it up and out of the water where he could wash it, spending extra time on her foot and toes. He repeated the same procedure on her right leg. Last, he reached into the water and nudged Morgan's thighs apart, so he could use the cloth on the area between them. Finally, he laid the washcloth on the side of the tub.

"You can open your eyes now." Stryker helped Morgan sit up and get out of the bathtub. He grabbed a clean towel and dried her off, including every small part. "Don't move." He stepped over to the door and came back with the terrycloth bathrobe to put on her. He put his arm around her, and they walked to the king-sized bed.

Morgan climbed on the bed first and lay on her back watching Stryker as he went around the bed to the other side and climbed in to kneel by her hips. He opened the robe and took a moment to admire Morgan's body before bending down with his head toward her feet. He reached under Morgan's upper thighs, pulled them apart, and slid his hands under her buttocks to lift her pelvis.

"Stryker, what are you doing?" Morgan asked with trepidation.

"You might like."

"Like what? Stryker?" Morgan started to protest but then Stryker lowered his mouth to Morgan's clitoris and began to swirl his tongue around the sensitive little organ. Morgan inhaled a quick breath, then exhaled, "Oh!"

Stryker continued using his tongue on her for over fifteen minutes, while Morgan tried to stifle the moans and sighs. She couldn't. He withdrew a hand from under and slid a finger inside. She was sloppy wet. Remembering Verity's instructions of years ago, he searched for the small rough spot, found it, and began caressing. He had not done this since being with Verity. *Hope I'm doing it right.*

Morgan began gyrating her hips. "Ahhh." She was into it.

Stryker then figured he must be doing okay.

Morgan's orgasm was about the strongest he had ever felt her have. She had two more and Stryker swung around to kiss her.

Morgan pulled her mouth away and said, "I want you inside me." When he entered her, she gasped, wrapped her legs around his hips, and then said, "Kiss me again."

Stryker moved her hand down to her clitoris and held it there until she began using it on herself. He didn't count. It took her three and a half hours, but he was sure she got into the high teens. He had three good ones himself. Afterward, while Morgan lay calming down, Stryker got off the bed and came back a minute later with a warm and wet washcloth. He attempted to apply it to Morgan's lips, but she stopped him with her hand. "It's okay, Stryker."

Later as they lay together on the bed, under the covers with Morgan's arm draped across Stryker's chest, and he was almost ready to fall asleep when Morgan demurely asked, "Stryker, if I'm ever bad, I mean really bad, do you suppose, I might have to be punished with another severe tongue lashing?"

ACKNOWLEDGMENTS

Thanks to Stacey Smekofske, my marvelous editor, and Linda Worker, my talented book cover artist.

ABOUT THE AUTHOR

Wes Rand was an Artillery Officer in the U.S. Army during the 1960s. He pays alimony. He doesn't like to golf but lives on a golf course. He has been bucked off a horse and two women.

He has a cabin in the mountains where he writes and hikes while his wife plays golf in Las Vegas. Wes enjoys living under the open skies in Nevada and Utah.

Follow Evil Stryker and Wes Rand at EvilStryker.com

facebook.com/wes.rand.14

instagram.com/rand.wes